THE WRECKING OF
OFFSHORE FIVE

The mine had lain undisturbed since the day in
1944 when it was jettisoned by a crashing aircraft. Now a trawler, fishing illicitly close to the
oil rig, jerked it free from the bottom; it broke
surface unseen in the fog and darkness. It
bobbed and spun, its horns swinging and pointing in search of a long awaited-victim. Currents
swept it towards Offshore Five.

Offshore Five was an old rig. Ten years old.
Seventy-one holes old. Holes as far apart as the
Caribbean and Indonesia. Some had discovered oil, one had found gas. Hole seventy-
two, out there on the Dogger Bank, might strike
the biggest bonanza ever. The North Sea
drilling stakes were high—at least £100,000,000
lost if nothing was found in truly commercial
quantities—many times more than that gained
if the rigs struck it rich.

Catastrophe, unpredictable as a thunderbolt,
strikes Offshore Five at a moment of crucial im-
portance in the search. To the Inoco oil
company it is vital that key information be
recovered from the wreck of the rig. . . .

In this high drama of shipwreck, rescue and
salvage Ronald Johnston develops his powers as
a gripping story-teller to their highest point;
his expert technical knowledge gives complete
authenticity to a story that is up-to-the-minute
in its setting and as old as the sea in its account of
the struggles of men against great natural forces.

THE WRECKING
OF
OFFSHORE FIVE

by

Ronald Johnston

584303/F

Collins
ST JAMES'S PLACE, LONDON

First Impression   February, 1967
Second Impression   June, 1967

Acknowledgements

I would like to thank those who provided me with information and advice when I was researching the background for this novel.

Mr. W. J. Browne of Petroleum Information Bureau.

Dr. T. F. Gaskell and Mr. John Collins of British Petroleum.

Lt.-Com. R. S. Bryden, M.B.E., D.S.C., R.N. (Retd.)

Lt.-Com. P. K. Kemp, O.B.E., R.N. (Retd.)

A special thank you goes to Lt.-Com. M. R. Todd, R.N., for his help and hospitality when I visited H.M.S. *Dolphin* at Gosport.

I would also like to acknowledge the advice given me then by the late Lt.-Com. R. Cudworth, R.N.

R.J.

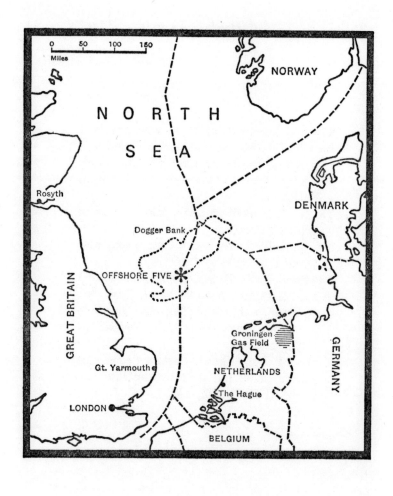

Chapter 1

It was big. It had lain undisturbed for more than twenty years since the day in 1944 when it was jettisoned. The plane had been unlucky. It was flying low in a typical North Sea overcast and came suddenly out into a patch of clear sky to find itself over a group of trawlers and an escorting corvette. The ships let fly with everything they had. In these waters at that time men in small ships had a special loathing for German planes. The bullets and shells tore great holes in the plane's belly, ripping open its fuel tanks, penetrating its engines. The pilot pulled back hard on the stick to gain height. He knew he would have to ditch but he meant to get rid of his load before he hit the water. The men on the trawlers grinned and shouted and gave each other thumbs up signs as they watched the swooping plane and growing feather of smoke trailing behind it. Then they saw the white parachutes blossoming against the scudding cloud. They thought it was the crew but the glasses told them it was mines. They counted as the feather grew to a great black smear which swept upwards, stopped abruptly as the stall came, then streaked downwards as the plane plunged into the sea.

The men cheered, then were silent. It was like that. The thrill of the chase soon dissipated when the quarry was dead. The men had counted carefully. Five years of war had taught them about mines. But they counted wrongly. They missed one mine. The sweepers had come out. They wanted to know about these mines. The Germans had not sown mines from the air since the first months of the war and then they had not been the contact type reported now. The sweepers cut loose and destroyed the mines. The number they got tallied with the number the little ships saw drop. It was a simple operation. They knew within a mile or two where the mines had fallen, they knew the number. What they had to find out was whether the mines had tripped clear of their sinkers and run out on their mooring wires. The sweeps soon gave confirmation as the wires were caught and cut and the mines broke surface, their horns still menacing but impotent against the warships' guns.

The one mine they missed did not separate from its sinker. Maybe the trip mechanism or the time switch had been jammed by the impact with the water when the parachute failed to open, maybe some slave worker had made a tiny contribution to the war by twisting a lever. Whatever the reason the mine and its sinker stayed locked together on the sand of the Dogger Bank. But no slave worker had been allowed near the explosive or the fuses or the final assembly. It was a very well-made mine, made to last, made to retain the destructive power of three-quarters of a ton of high explosive for a lifetime. It had stayed there on the bottom for more than twenty years. The swirling currents which scoured and carried and replaced the sand had cocooned the mine. Trawls passed close, some right over the spot, but the sand had clung to its secret.

Then the oil rig came to probe the earth's crust under the sea. The three huge legs were wound down on to the Bank and spudded into the sand and shale and clay. Then the platform was jacked up fifty feet above the grey water, the drilling gear was set up and the tungsten tipped bit was lowered to the sea bed and began chewing out a hole in the sand and rock. The rig had already drilled three holes. Each time it moved its great legs to a new location, the local currents changed direction because of the alien obstructions. Where they had scoured sand from, now they laid it down.

Where once they had piled it up, now they scoured it out. And the mine was uncovered.

The trawler had no right to be there. There was a recommended clearance of three miles round all offshore rigs. But the trawler skipper was hunting fish and he thought he knew where he could find them. Regulations meant little to him when he was on to a big shoal. Anyway, no one should know this time; it was dark and the mist patches were thick, low on the water and frequent. The patrol boat from the rig might come sniffing around but it would only bawl through its loud hailer. With any luck the trawler would be through the circle before anyone noticed.

The trawl board scraped along the bottom sand and snagged under the sinker of the mine. The weight of the tow from the steaming trawler came down through the trawl rope and jerked the sinker free from its grave. The jerk freed the mine and it rose lazily on the end of its wire. The rotted wire caught in the sharp angle of the steel-shod board and was snipped clean through. The buoyancy of the mine brought it up quickly to break surface unseen in the wake of the fishing boat, already lost in the fog and the darkness.

The mine bobbed and spun in the wake and the surface currents, its horns swinging and pointing as if in search of a long awaited victim. It lay low in the water. The wake of the trawler subsided and the surface currents took hold. It was less than a mile to the rig and the currents here ran strongly.

Offshore Five was an old rig. Ten years old. Seventy-one holes old. Holes as far apart as the Caribbean and Indonesia. Holes as deep as eighteen thousand feet down inside the earth. Fourteen of these holes had discovered oil in commercial quantities; one of them had probed out a vast reservoir of natural gas. Hole seventy-two, out there on the Dogger Bank, might strike the biggest bonanza of them all. Or it might be dry and a pointer to a losing

9

gamble in the rush to find oil under the North Sea. The stakes were high—at least £100,000,000 lost if nothing was ever found in truly commercial quantities—many times more than that gained if the rigs struck it really rich.

Inoco, the American oil combine, owned Offshore Five. They were building two more rigs, one on the Clyde, the other on the North East coast. They had towed Offshore Five half-way round the world to make a start on the North Sea search. They were drilling now out on the extreme edge of the British zone. They were looking for proof of a new and startling theory. They wanted that proof before deciding whether to lease the whole northern part of the Dutch sector. There was not much time left. The Dutch options had only three days to run.

It was an anxious time for everyone. A broken drill pipe, a generator failure, a sudden storm, a hundred uncontrollable chances could cost a fortune. It was worst of all for Edward Colney, the geologist whose original thinking had produced the unique structure theory, who had been on Offshore Five for six months now, who for sixteen hours of every day, seven days a week, peered through his microscope at the rock chippings pouring up in the drillers mud from thousands of feet below. He peered, he tested, he recorded, he compared. He chafed even at the necessary delays; coupling new lengths of drill pipe, changing the drill bit, casing in the hole with steel and cement. He was a man wholly dedicated to his science; he had ideas about the North Sea and he was in a hurry to prove them.

The tide was setting west by south at half a knot. On that course the mine would pass north of the rig. But the tide was fickle hereabouts. It changed direction and speed every hour. The fog was thicker than ever. It swirled and fumed, one moment blanketing all vision, the next opening a clear sight for a hundred yards in one direction, then rolling it shut to give a momentary clear patch in another.

The foghorn on the rig blared at regular intervals. All the lights were haloed in fog; the red warning lights all round at deck level, the porthole lights from the cabins and the recreation rooms, the winking red lights two hundred feet above the water to warn off aircraft, and the brilliant arc lamps lighting the drilling platform. The work went on in all weathers, day and night. Work meant noise and that September evening the noise rose to crescendoes then faded as the banks of fog caught it and multiplied it and smothered it like a mute moving in and out of the end of a trumpet.

Close to, the noise was unmuted, even intensified by the pall of fog. The huge drilling winch clattered, wires hummed with the weight of thousands of feet of pipe suspended from them, chains shrieked and clanked as they whipped round drill pipes, unscrewing three pieces at a time in a stand of ninety feet, to be winched away and stacked upright inside the derrick. Pumps roared, generators throbbed, tools rang on steel, boots clumped and slithered on wet gratings, and the foghorn blared. The one noise that was missing was the sound of voices. Each man knew his job, the timing was perfect. One mistake could mean death or mangling. And time was money. It said so in printed notices outside and inside, everywhere on the rig. Time Is Money, and Don't Talk, Don't Ask, Don't Remember—these were the commandments on Offshore Five.

On and around the drilling platform the night shift worked like demons. Hand signals controlled every operation. The shift toolpusher watched every move, ready to tongue lash the first man who made a mistake. It was not necessary. The roughnecks and roustabouts knew their jobs—they were on the rig for the money—no shop steward would protect them there—one mistake and out. They were all Geordies or Scots, all except the toolpusher, he was American. Offshore Five had three Americans aboard, the two shift toolpushers and the boss of the rig, Brad Tucker. He was out there now waiting for the core barrel to come up out of the depths.

He was a big man, over six feet, two hundred and twenty pounds, and all muscle. He had been in oil for forty years, starting as a kid of sixteen back home. He had seen it all. He never spoke unless he had something that needed saying. He was the antithesis of the caricaturist's loud mouthed Texan. He thought a lot and that heavy-featured expressionless face concealed a shrewd mind and an iron will. He had strong feelings about a lot of things but about nothing more than scientific oilmen. Sure, they had their place. Seismic surveys, geological charts, lab tests of samples, it was all a help. But making hole was the only real answer to finding oil. And drilling was his job. He had made hole across the world; in the past fifteen years nearly all offshore. On the rig, he was boss. He made the decisions, he took the credit, he took the kicks. At least that was how it had been for the last ten years on Offshore Five. Until this time. This time he had Colney with his secret theories and the ear of the head man in London. Theories. Three dry holes and this one down to fifteen thousand feet and showing nothing. Not just straightforward dry holes but holes drilled with special tests and solid core samples all the way down, holes drilled through thousands of feet of salt with all the trouble that brought, holes drilled day and night, every day, in all the fog and gales and raw cold the North Sea could muster. And that was some, even in summer. When Brad Tucker spoke Colney's name he said it like a dirty word.

He stood there on the edge of the drilling floor watching his men work. The wet air glistened on their oilskins and condensed on their faces to mingle with the running sweat. The noise was stunning. The men worked well. They were his big success on Offshore Five. Men who six months before had been seamen, coal miners, shipbuilders. Now they were oilmen and he had performed the miracle of change. He hunched down into his coat till he felt the fur collar damp but comforting on his neck. He could see droplets of water hanging on the peak of his leather storm cap. He shook his head to clear them off then nodded as the toolpusher signalled one more stand of pipe to draw.

The winch clattered and wires sang as the last section came up. The locking wrenches swung in and grasped the pipe, the pipe was spun free, two roustabouts threw round the hauling wire and the drill pipe swung away to join the huge stack against the derrick frame. Up on the safety platform, the spidermen unclamped the tongs and signalled all clear. The tongs came down fast on the end of the travelling block, roughnecks guided them on to the end of the core barrel still held rigid in its wrench. Wrench off, take the weight, hold it, break out the locking collar from the turntable, heave away. The block and the tongs rose and up came the core barrel, holding inside its eight-foot length a solid sample of the earth from fifteen thousand feet below. Drillers' mud dripped and oozed everywhere. The coring bit was up through the turntable. Off came the bit and the lower end of the barrel was capped. Lower away. Tongs off and cap the other end.

Two of the men carried the core off the drilling floor, along the deck and up the ladder to the geology hut. Tucker followed and took it from them outside the hut. He held it upright in one of his great fists as if it weighed no more than a walking-stick. Even before he pressed the buzzer button, the noise had started up again under the derrick. A new bit was being sent down the hole to be followed by almost three miles of drill pipe. He stabbed the button again. This place affronted him. Since Offshore Five was built, geologists had made do with a portable shack or a caravan type trailer. But that was not good enough for Colney. He had to have this contraption. It had been made ashore and welded into position when the rig was being refitted for the North Sea. It was a laboratory in a steel box. There were no windows or portholes. Colney worked in fluorescent light; he said that that way he always had exactly the same illumination. There was a small bathroom and a fold-up bed at one end of the lab.

Colney lived here; he worked here, he slept here, ate here. It was bare of human comforts except books but its own air conditioning plant kept it snug and warm. It was well soundproofed; only the barest sensation of the harsh noise of the rig penetrated here. Tucker had christened it Colney Hatch when he heard of the lunatic association.

He pressed the buzzer again, holding it in and glaring at the red light above the door forbidding entry. This was the craziest bit of the arrangement. There was this outside door which led into a sort of sealed vestibule. From there another door led into the lab. Colney was most meticulous in his drill for opening and shutting these doors. The two doors and the vestibule between were a precaution against gusts of wind and spray blowing into the laboratory and against anyone entering unannounced. Tucker thought it was to protect the geologist from contact with the outside air. The red light changed to green and the handles on the door were turned from the inside.

Tucker watched as each of the lever type handles moved, then the door swung out a few inches and a wedge of light cut through the gloom. Colney's face appeared momentarily, his nose twitching as if offended by some odour, eyes screwed up and blinking behind the black-framed glasses. The face withdrew and Tucker pulled open the door and stepped inside. The geologist nodded excitedly and rubbed his hands when he saw the core. He pulled the door shut and carefully locked off each of the handles before opening the other door into the laboratory.

The Texan stepped through in front of Colney. When he thought about it Tucker was always amazed at the satisfaction he got from being ill-mannered with Colney. It was not a natural trait. He dumped the core on one of the benches.

"There it is, Limey." He always used that name. He knew it annoyed the Englishman. They had to see each other every day and for six months the slanging match had been building up.

The geologist said nothing till he sealed off the inside door. "You took long enough getting it, Tucker."

Brad stiffened. He was not one to bother about formal titles. From the men he took Skipper, Mate, Boss, Squire. He had even laughed at a rhymer from the Fife coalfield who described him by repeating his name with just the first letter altered. But this bare, English way of using a surname alone—that struck deep against his informal American roots. He sniffed and got that faintest smell of chemicals that the air conditioner never wholly scoured away. He unhooked the phone from the wall and buzzed the wireless room.

"Brad here. What's new?"

The radio man told him that Mr. Bright had been on from London wanting the latest news.

"Can't disappoint Brightboy, can we? Tell him we've got a core at fifteen thousand. The genius is working on it now." He hooked up the phone. The message would go out on the radio telephone in that day's plain language code just in case any snoopers were listening in. "D'you hear that, Limey? Your pal in London's biting his nails for news. Do I tell him it's another of your dry holes?"

Colney said nothing He already had the core out of the steel tube. It lay on the bench, gleaming in the light. He lined it up with the saw and switched on. The quiet of the laboratory was shattered with the screech of the high-speed motor. He set the guide clamps and fed the core on to the whirling blade. The pitch of the motor dropped and was almost drowned by the rasp of the teeth slicing through the rock, splitting the core up its length into two half-rounds.

Tucker watched. Seeing Colney at work was seeing pure devotion. He was a small man, lightly built. He looked a weakling but anyone who had tried him with a crushing handshake knew that these arms and the long-fingered hands were like tempered steel. Now, bent over his core sample, feeding it lovingly into the saw, his eyes all-seeing through the big spectacles, he was like a hunter with his prey square in the sights. Brad shook his head. You had to admire the guy even if you wouldn't ever admit it to his face. Maybe even envy him. He had no problems like ordinary men. This was his whole life. All he wanted to do was to find out about the inside of the earth. Six months he had been on Offshore Five. Never a day ashore. Nothing to go ashore for. His world was underneath the surface not on top of it. Even if his theories were a lot of balls, you still had to admire him.

The screeching saw stopped. The core lay on the bench in its two eight-foot halves. Colney was marking it with a felt pen. He moved slowly along the bench peering at the cut surfaces of the sample. He made notes. He went back and examined it all again, this time with a magnifier. He pulled down a note-book from a shelf and studied some entries. He stood up straight and took off his glasses. He polished them carefully with a tissue.

"I suggest another three hundred feet and a new core," he said.

"You've got to be kidding," roared Tucker. "What is this? Some sort of egghead joke?"

"Three hundred feet and another core, Tucker."

"Look, Limey," growled the Texan, walking over and stabbing his finger into Colney's chest. "I'm here to make hole. I've cut more cores for you than I've cut for any man in forty years of drilling. I'm getting tired. What've you got there that's so wonderful?" He turned and glared up and down the length of the sample. "Hell, I'm no Doctor of Science but I know enough to know there ain't no hydro-carbons in that lot."

"Quite right. But, as you say, you're not a Doctor of Science. I have been for more than ten years. Three hundred feet and a fresh core."

Tucker was angry. "You're starting to annoy me, Limey." He pulled a carton of cigars from his jacket and ripped the cellophane off one.

"I don't mean to upset you, Tucker. It's just that sometimes our interests seem to be opposed. But you said it yourself. Roger Bright's biting his nails for news." He paused then added, "I'd rather you didn't smoke in here."

Tucker drew himself up to his full height, and glared down at the little geologist. "All right, Limey. Three hundred feet and a core. If that's what you and Brightboy want, that's what you'll get." He struck a match and held it close to Colney's face. "Right now, what I want is a smoke. And I'm bloody well going to have it." He raised the match and blew a fragrant cloud down over the other man's face.

Outside the fog was thinning with the coming of a breeze. The tide had backed to south-west. The mine was now drifting on line of target. The target was Offshore Five.

Chapter 2

The lights were on in the top floor of the Inoco Building in London. The top floor had been given to Inoco Exploration (U.K.) because it was the newest subsidiary and the older departments were glad to be free of the architectural oversight which stopped the express lifts one floor short of the top story. This suited the exploration company very well. Security was the biggest problem. This way, with everyone having to approach by a single stairway, it was possible to check staff and visitors with great care. Everyone was happy, even the architects and contractors with whom Inoco had been wrangling over the omission ever since the building was put up. The architects had always claimed that a truly private suite of offices had obvious advantages though they had never been able to be specific. Inoco was pleased to let the whole thing drop and get on with the business of finding, transporting, refining and selling oil.

The top floor suited Roger Bright. He liked the view and he liked the separateness. Lower down the geography of the building became confused and it was difficult to avoid meeting people you had no desire to see and getting involved in company politics which might be about some trivial thing like trying to grab extra office space or a major problem such as how to ensure your next step on the promotion ladder.

There were those who would confide that Roger's distaste for such manœuvring only confirmed that he had no need to indulge in it. He had acquired his own golden ladder when he married Paula Hartz. Her father was on the board in New York. This did Roger less than justice. He was certainly ambitious but his Brightboy nickname was earned among oilmen before he met Paula. Those who knew their Inoco knew that Paula might turn out to be one of his few major errors of judgment.

Roger Bright was thirty-five. Young men often have senior posts in oil but as managing director of Inoco's North Sea project he had a very big job indeed. It was big not just because of the millions invested or the vast prizes to be won or lost, but because of the nature of the thing. It was the biggest gamble the oil business had ever taken. Bright was in overall charge of the whole project as well as the drilling in the British licence blocks. The site they were working on butted on to the Dutch sector and Piet van Sluys of Inoco N.V. had options on both the northern and southern areas. They could have one or the other, not both. The fall of the Dutch government over that offshore television station had held up final leasing but that might prove a happy coincidence if Offshore Five's tests were completed on schedule. Bright would then know better which Dutch leases to take. Time and timing were all important. Time Is Money.

The way to the top for Bright had not been a bed of roses though, until he left university, life had been comfortable and uncomplicated if humdrum. He was what the English call better middle class. His father had been an insurance broker, his mother a journalist on a women's weekly. She had taken six weeks off to have Roger. They lived in Surrey, not in the stockbroker belt but near enough to bask in its reflection. With both parents working, the boy had gone to prep school when he was seven. It cost little more than the nanny he had grown up with till then. His father had been in one of the City territorial units and was killed early in the war. He left a small trust fund for his son. Roger went on to public school. His mother was doing well, she was an editor now and they were still quite well off. The war finished and four years later Roger went from school to Cambridge. He liked Varsity, He rowed, played cricket, went to parties, and did some work. He left with a very ordinary degree and after half a dozen interviews was taken on by Inoco under a management training scheme.

Just then his mother died. It was sudden and unexpected. They had spent most of their lives apart but there had been a special sort of bond between them. To him she had been a symbol of safety and succour. When he needed money, she found it for him. When he needed excuses, she provided them. She had always been there in the background to soften the harshness of growing up. For her, he was proof that she was fulfilled, a married woman, a mother, and a career woman; the kind of character who peopled the pages of the women's weekly she edited. He was someone to boast of, to spoil, to ignore when more urgent things came up. He was good-looking too, just like the highly coloured illustrations in her magazine.

Her death dropped him suddenly into reality. There was some money but not much. There were now no ties. He was on his own. He started to work. The interviewers and psychologists who had talked to him and tested him when he started with Inoco were staggered by the reports that came back. The idea was to pass trainees from one department to another to broaden their experience and discover their special talents. Roger went through the departments and on every one he left his mark. The refinery, road tankers, sales, personnel, publicity, franchise service stations, he took them all in his stride. He was as enthusiastic scraping sludge from a storage tank as he was sarcastic criticising a new sales campaign. The computer which processed personnel records gave him a remarkable rating. He was sent to America.

The parent company took everything from Britain with a pinch of salt so the process started all over again. Cleaning tanks, wiping windscreens, drilling, surveying, accountancy, selling. The results were impressive. They sent him to Harvard to the Business School and he left there with a report that made even the hard-headed men in New York sit up and take notice. Brightboy was a name being whispered where decisions were made. Down to Texas for experience drilling offshore, over to Venezuela, then out to the Middle East for his first job on his own. It was there he first met Ted Colney. Colney's ideas and Roger's push had brought in the biggest offshore strike ever in the Persian Gulf. Back to New York for another vetting and the news that he was being given the North Sea. Bright had proved that English public school and university overlaid with American drive and know-how was a formidable background.

That time in New York he met Paula. He met and married her in six weeks. Even at the time he wondered why he did it. He was in love with her but that was not the kind of reason he would admit to himself. She already had one divorce and quite a reputation. He wondered if it was the reaction after the heat and stench and celibacy of the Gulf. She certainly cured his celibacy. Paula was an enthusiast in bed. He told himself afterwards that he got the North Sea without her father's help but there was always a nagging doubt. Paula got what she wanted; she wanted Europe. For her, Europe, sophistication and civilisation were all synonymous. She was soaking up her civilisation now down on the Italian coast.

He got up from his desk and walked over to the window. From there, the West End, the City, and the river lay like a map below, etched in street lights and neons. It was as if he was literally on top of the world. He smiled at the thought. He knew what a precarious perch that was, especially with the options soon to fall due on these Dutch leases and no definite findings from Offshore Five. He lit a cigarette and opened the folding map panels on the wall. The map showed the whole North Sea area split into the sections claimed by each of the countries surrounding it. In the British area most of the southern part was already leased in blocks of a hundred square miles. The map was marked with coloured symbols showing exactly which company held the rights in each block. Out on the eastern boundary, on the Dogger Bank, was the series of red blocks that Offshore Five was working. Inoco had other blocks but they would not be explored until the new rigs were delivered. Shaded parts in the Dutch zone showed where van Sluys had the options for Inoco N.V. If it all worked out, they would have a huge piece of sea bed all to themselves, either north or south.

This was what Roger Bright wanted. Elsewhere you were hedged round with competitors' blocks and this meant that if you made a strike, your competitors would soon be drilling down to tap off a share of your find. A big area had tremendous advantages but only if you made a strike. And it would have to be a big strike for out there, in the middle of the sea, transport and operating costs were astronomical.

Roger ran his eye over the map checking off the legends which summarised all his intelligence reports on other companies' drilling. North and west of Offshore Five there were several dry holes with persistent rumours that one had had a small show of oil. There were Offshore Five's own three dry holes with nothing but Colney's confident predictions to make them worthwhile.

Well, he told himself, we'll see what this one produces. Just wish I knew more about Ted's theory. That's his way, though. He gives no details till he's sure. But if he says there might be oil there, I trust him. He's been right far more often than he's been wrong. If he says he's on to a unique structure, he probably is. Seismic reports suggest thousands of feet of solid salt. The only unique thing about that is the unique cost of drilling. But that reserves calculation of Ted's is tantalising. Ten times the breakeven figure. He shook his head. It was all contrary to accepted ideas. All the confirmed strikes in the North Sea area had been natural gas. First Groningen, then offshore neaɪ the Dutch and German coast. There had been several small, useless finds farther out in the German zone and, last year, the British strikes off the East Coast. The odds were on gas being found elsewhere. Was that why Ted Colney insisted he could find oil? He was an odd character. His favourite comment was: "If it's accepted theory, I start by doubting it."

Bright pushed the map panels shut. The whole North Sea was one huge gamble. He felt justified in backing an outsider in this first race when he knew the form so well. It was a calculated risk; he had already calculated how to cover it. If Colney failed to prove his theory by the time these options fell due in three days, Roger would take him off the rig, let the northern options lapse, and plump for the popular south. Colney was expendable if he was not finding oil. But Roger desperately wanted him to find oil. Gas would only be a second best with all the problems of an undeveloped market, new equipment, new capital, new techniques. And here in Britain a nationalised monopoly calling the tune on prices and conditions.

The controller came in with a message from the rig. There were three controllers. They kept a round the clock vigil, one always on duty.

"What's this, Tom?" asked Bright.

"It's a message from Offshore Five, sir."

Bright took it and translated it. They had taken a core sample at fifteen thousand feet. No report yet on it from Colney. "What's the weather like out there?"

"It's foggy but starting to clear. The outlook's pretty grim, wind and rain."

"The outlook's always grim out there."

The other man went out and Bright entered up the report in the log-book and locked it away. One of the phones rang on his desk. It was the outside line. He picked it up, wondering if it was Paula. She sometimes rang about this time; she got a conscience about her husband when she reached the fourth Martini.

"Bright."

"Roger, my boy, how are you?"

"Bearing up." He recognised the deep fruity voice and the precise, accented English of van Sluys.

"Piet van Sluys here."

"I had realised," said Roger, smiling. Piet was twenty years his senior but never seemed to be offended by working under him. He had been in oil all his life and had provided a fund of advice on this North Sea project from the beginning. Roger could visualise him now in his office in The Hague, his great body lying back in an arm-chair, his booted feet perched up on the desk to take the weight off his paunch, and his waistcoat powdered with ash from the cigar which was always in his mouth. "What do you want, you great gin drinking Dutchman?"

Van Sluys chuckled. "Are you scrambled, Roger?"

Bright pressed the scrambler switch on the phone. If there was a wire tap it would now be useless. "I'm on, Piet. What's so important?"

"It's about these options. We've only got three days left."

"I know that." Bright was curt. "I told you I'd be in touch."

"I know, Roger. There's no need to get shirty. I just wanted to remind you that I don't like that northern area. I know your Mr. Colney is a genius but our seismic work shows far better prospects farther south. And you know all the problems of active exploration."

Yes, thought Bright. I know all the problems. These leases will insist on planned programmes which will keep the two new rigs fully employed in whichever area we choose. That means there's only Offshore Five to work the British blocks. And rigs are in such demand there's no hope of renting one. It's not just the licence fees, it's the rigs each ringing up a bill for £7,000 a day, seven days a week.

24

Two new rigs plus Offshore Five. Three rigs. £21,000 a day. A million pounds every six or seven weeks. And that's not the most important thing. The important thing is whether they make a strike. And if it's a commercial strike. And if they don't make a strike, would they have made one somewhere else. Yes, I know all the problems.

"Are you still there, Roger?"

"Yes, Piet. Sorry. I was thinking. Don't worry, I'm not in a hurry to make a fool of myself. If I don't get the test results I want, you can have your pet blocks in the south."

"Fine, Roger. Thank you. I just wanted to be sure you knew how I feel."

"That's all right, Piet. You know I value your advice. I'll be in touch. 'Bye."

He laid down the phone. Piet van Sluys was another who did not trust Colney. Everyone was very free with advice. Bright grimaced. It's easy to hand out advice when you're not making the decisions.

Two miles south of the rig the workboat was turning back to her usual patrol. *Circe* was based on an American tug design with a high island bridge set forward of midships. It was not the ideal shape for the North Sea but the long uncluttered deck and hold space aft was good for handling stores. Her two big diesels gave her ample power and a fair turn of speed. She handled like a dream and though the old salts along the harbour at Yarmouth shook their heads, Johnny Ellam was in love with her. Sailors usually feel that way about their first command.

Ellam had been in the Inoco tanker fleet since he finished his apprenticeship. A good officer, still single and footloose, he had planned to drift out to the Far East after he got Master's and indulge his romantic notions of the China Coast and the Pacific. He had been told that Maugham was out of date but he wanted a change. The chance of *Circe* came just after he got Master's. He was still numb

25

from his celebrations and the idea of his own ship working with the offshore rigs was novel. He accepted and postponed his plans to take Hong Kong and Tahiti by storm.

A lot of the work was routine. Taking supplies to the rig, taking crews to and from the rig, acting as a diving tender for the frogmen checking on the rig's legs, chugging round and round in circles keeping an eye open for the snoopers the other oil companies sent out. But to have his own ship was still thrill enough and it could be fun when you caught a snooper as *Circe* just had.

Johnny sat in his swing chair in the wheelhouse wiping the tears of laughter from his eyes. "Jesus," he gasped, "that's the best yet." Come to think of it, security's the funniest thing about this whole carry-on. Every bar and club you go into ashore, people start buying you drinks and stroking your thighs to see if you've got any information that's worth buying. Half the whores on the east coast must be working for the oil companies nowadays. Then there are the spies on the rig, taking their money from Inoco and selling every rumour they can pick up to competitors. And there are the boats. Small boats, big boats, fishing boats, motor cruisers like that one, all full of binoculars and radio gear, some even say frogmen, all trying to find some little gem of news about what's going on, on that ugly steel island

Ellam lit a cigarette and thought about that cruiser. He had picked up two ships on the radar, north-east and south-west of Offshore Five. He had had to choose. The one to the north-east was steaming away at about seven knots, the other one was stationary. He put the moving one down as a trawler, inside the recommended distance but fishing. Good luck to him. Why should Inoco hold up the supply of fish and chips? He swung round and headed south-west. *Circe* and the cruiser played hide-and-seek in the fog banks for half an hour before they met in a clear patch. Johnny switched on the searchlight to have a good look, It was a beautiful boat, its white paint glowing in the light, just like any other cruiser but for being half-way across the North Sea and dangling aerials along its length.

A loud-hailer barked. "Put out that damned light. What the devil d'you think you're doing?"

Johnny lifted the microphone. "If you don't like the illuminations, go find a dark corner."

"What ship's that? Don't order me about or I'll report you." The voice sounded military through the metallic amplification.

Ellam grinned. So some redundant army officer's had to find a job. "That was no order. That was a threat. Now get going, mate, or I'll push you."

A foul instruction leapt across the water.

Johnny took the wheel himself and pushed the engine controls to full speed. *Circe* surged forward, turning to head for the cruiser. Fifty feet away he spun the wheel and the workboat sheared off, flinging her wake under the spy boat. The cruiser jumped and rolled under the impact. Curses crackled in the air. Ellam grinned and spun the wheel again to turn *Circe* round. The cruiser had started up and was already heading west. Ellam came round alongside and matched her speed. The searchlight was still on the boat.

"That's right, mate, run home to your mam."

"Bloody madman."

Johnny had not thought about the foam gun. But it was there and he was in the mood for fun. He tipped it down and squeezed the trigger for a three-second burst. The cockpit of the cruiser disappeared in a mound of foam. Splutterings came from the loud-hailer as the foam oozed and slithered down over the superstructure. A door flew open and an irate figure was enveloped in the last cascade of froth sliding off the cockpit roof. Ellam was hysterical with mirth. He staggered back into the wheelhouse and spun *Circe* away to port. He throttled back the engines, gave the wheel back to the man on watch and collapsed in his chair. The cruiser was at full speed, going away,

27

Johnny swivelled his chair and studied the radar. The rig showed huge on the screen, the trawler was away to the north-east and the cruiser was trailing west. Nothing else. He switched down to short range and steadied *Circe* on course. He reported back to Offshore Five on the R/T and had a new fit of laughter when the radio man said he hoped it really had been a spy boat. That's even better. Some poor spare-time sailor scurrying westwards to escape a nightmare.

The fog was thinning in front of the breeze. The rig's lights showed clearly above the patches then the stark silhouette grew downwards to the water as the workboat came nearer and the mist was stirred and blown away. Ellam went round the rig to the east. It was when he was turning west again that he saw the radar echo close up to Offshore Five.

He watched it, switching ranges and tuning the clutter switch. The echo was intermittent but it was an echo. He took the glasses and peered into the darkness under the rig. Black as pitch. He swore quietly and brought the boat round to head close in. When would they ever learn? No gash to be dumped from the rig. That was the rule but there was always some joker ready to drop a drum of galley gash over the side. Ah well, it breaks the monotony. No sea to speak of. It'll be easy to manœuvre close to, net the drum and haul it on board. He throttled back and alerted the deck watch. It was a regular chore. He knew he only had to put the boat in the right position and the crew would do the rest. *Circe* came in close to the rig and Ellam switched on the searchlight.

The noise of the winches and the pumps and the clatter from the drilling platform beat down and drowned the rhythmic thudding of the boat's engines. At first he saw nothing but the dark water swirling round the rig's legs and the drill pipe spinning. As the boat moved alongside he got a clear sight between two of the legs.

"Christ." He had never seen a mine before. In pictures,

28

yes, but never in the water. For a second he froze. Then his brain started chasing memories from films and books. You fire at them. They sink or blow up. Can't do that under the rig. Haven't got a gun anyway. You tow them away to a safe place. Tow them, that means a line. Who dares put a line on one of these? Lasso them. And maybe break the fuse in one of these horns. God's truth.

Circe was almost abreast of the mine now. Have to try and get hold of it. Hard-a-starboard. Port half ahead, starboard full astern. Turn her round. Back up to it. He ran to the port wing. The deck lights were on aft. The watch was there, all staring aft. There was terror in their stillness. The boat was turning fast. The confused water from the screws drifted white on the dark water, spinning the mine, pushing it out of reach under Offshore Five. Damn and blast. But that's it. That's how to do it. Wash it clear with the wake. It's a chance. Take a chance and pray. Engines both astern. *Circe* steadied and surged aft. Her stern was right under the rig now. Full ahead both. The water boiled under her stern. Ellam watched, his heart beating wildly and cold sweat prickling on his neck. The boat jumped ahead and the wake streamed out and pushed the mine through under the rig to the other side. It was working. Now hard over and round to the other side. As the mine comes clear, run between it and the rig, washing it farther away. Then again and so on till it's well clear. Then sit and watch it till someone arrives who knows what to do. Hold your horses, Johnny boy. You're not out of the wood yet. What was it that Scots skipper used to say? "When the one o'clock gun hits the bullseye, then we'll be out of the forest, then we'll be out of the wood." Not yet. Christ, I haven't warned the rig.

As the helmsman spun the wheel to take *Circe* round, Johnny pulled the klaxon lever. The raucous wail cut through all the other sound like a scream in church. It was five seconds before its sister sirens on the rig joined in, amplified through the loudspeakers to every compartment of Offshore Five. The drilling winch stopped, the spinning pipe came to rest, the men on the platform stood where they were, not knowing what it all meant. In cabins and messes, in the generator room and the radio shack, in the galley and in the geology lab, men stopped, listened, wondered, then jerked into terrified action.

Ellam knew his problem was not solved as soon as he rounded the angle of the rig. The searchlight showed the mine wallowing near the leg at the apex of the triangular island. He made up his mind. Have to take a chance. Go right underneath at full speed. That'll wash it clear. There's a fifty foot clearance under there. That's enough. He steadied *Circe* at full speed. The little ship sped straight at Offshore Five. Ellam saw that the mine was much nearer the leg than he had thought. Too late now. *Circe* plunged under the platform, the whip aerial above the bridge bending as it struck and scraped along the underside. The mine was only a few feet clear of the starboard side. The noise was deafening under there, the klaxon still screaming and reverberating off the steel plates.

Out on the other side the noise of the klaxon dropped only to be joined by the sound of the sirens on the rig. *Circe* leaned over as she turned under full rudder and Ellam looked back down the beam of the searchlight. It had worked. The mine was going clear. He blew breath through his teeth and the taut muscles of his jaw relaxed. The relief was short lived The backlash of the wake caught the mine and sucked it back. He watched, helpless, as the mine wallowed in the turbulent water then, caught in another eddy, hurled itself against the huge lattice leg.

Chapter 3

The explosion tore a great gap out of the leg. It was severed for all but a few steel ties. Ellam saw the huge upheaval of water first, then he felt the blast buffeting him like a warm wind, and immediately the sound was on him. It was deep, in a way muffled, but growing in volume till it overwhelmed all else and stunned the ears. As the roar faded to a rumble, then a murmur, he felt the shock waves, through the water, into every plate and plank of *Circe*, and up into his feet and hands where they touched the deck and rails. After the momentary deafness he began to pick up other sounds, water lapping, the phut-phut of the exhaust from the funnel close behind him, his breath rasping in his throat.

He stared down the beam of the searchlight. His hand felt for the controls to stop the engines, then the klaxon lever and the scream above his head died abruptly. Offshore Five was still there, miraculously erect. Her lights glowed brightly in the sharp clear air that follows fog. Johnny could see where the mine had almost amputated the leg. He stared dumbfounded at the rig standing there on its two undamaged legs for what seemed an age. It was only seconds. He was suddenly aware of new sounds. Steel on steel, metal in torment, voices shouting. *Circe* seemed much nearer the rig. The derrick looked higher but the base was the same distance off. He could see over the edge of the helicopter deck. The gap in the leg had closed. It's coming down. The whole bloody thing's coming down. And right across my ship. He leapt backwards and rammed both engine controls to full astern. He held on to the levers with both hands, willing *Circe* to back up fast.

On the rig the explosion ended the mystery of the sirens. No one had known what they meant except that they meant danger. These men had lived their working lives in danger, on ships, in coal-mines, in oil fields, but this was a new kind of danger, imminent but unknown. The men on the drilling floor stood still listening to the sirens and feeling the throb of the pumps and the generators. Up on the safety platform the two spidermen peered down into the wedge of light below. They saw the workboat disappearing under the rig. Its klaxon was blaring. The rig's sirens were screaming. The boat must be out of control carrying on like that. Hold on for that bump. It's only a wee boat. The rig'll stand up grand to a dunt from that. Awfy din about awfy little.

Below decks, men woke up, men stopped eating, playing cards, throwing darts, talking. The noise from the loudspeakers was deafening, paralysing in the enclosed spaces. For seconds they sat, stood, lay where they were, then the meaning got through to them. They grabbed clothes, shoes, lifejackets, and ran for doors. They jostled in the alleyways and on the stairs, some shouted questions, some bawled orders.

Only in the galley were the sirens ignored. That cook had been at sea. He knew all about fire and boat drills. He had been skipping them for more years than he cared to remember. He had always got away with it. "Sorry, sir, but I knew you'd understand. It's my bread, y'see. Can't leave my bread in the ovens." This time it was his soup. He was proud of his soup. Fruit juice, that was all right for Yanks; but soup, that was what these Geordies and Fifers wanted. Not just tinned soup, watered down, but real soup full of meat and vegetables and barley and lentils, all brewed up in thick marrow-bone stock. Rib-sticking soup. He was skimming the fat off the cauldron. To hell with them sirens.

In the radio shack the operator listened and waited. Someone would tell him. It might be a short circuit. Brad Tucker would tell him soon. He watched the light on the phone and held the headset tight over his ears to shut out the screaming sirens.

In the lab, Tucker had just stubbed out his cigar. Colney was bent over the core, prising out a specimen for his microscope. He coughed again as the last puff of cigar smoke wreathed round his head. The sirens brought his head up with a jerk. He stared at the loudspeaker, surprised and frightened. Brad listened and counted. If it was a short it would cut in five seconds. Four—Five—Six. He ran for the door. He grabbed the handgrip and pulled. The swing handles kept it shut. He swore and started fisting the levers free. Crazy bloody door. Crazy bloody Colney.

The blast of the mine hit the underside of the rig and shuddered along and up through every beam and bulkhead, every plate and strut. Everyone stopped. They felt it and heard it. What was it? The hole? No sign at the turntable. What then? Everything seemed all right. The lights had flickered but were still on. The pumps still thudded, the generators whined, the sirens shrieked. Then slowly the deck canted, imperceptibly at first, then more steeply. Straining, sundering metal started to sound. Now the men knew all they needed to know. Offshore Five was going in.

On the drilling floor men grasped for handholds, their feet slithering on the slanting deck, treacherous with damp and drillers' mud. They looked round desperately for ways of escape, not just escape over the side but escape from tools and stores careering down the slope. A spare drilling bit, huge, fearsome with its thousands of teeth exposed, slid and sparked across the plates, bounding off obstructions, demolishing, making men jump for their lives. One of the massive locking wrenches swung free, scything down one man and pinning another by his arm. Then came sacks of cement, casing pipes, hand tools, bundles of chain, oil drums. As the angle grew, the stands of drill pipe stacked on end waiting to be fed back down the hole broke their holding chains and toppled. They fell in a tangled mass. They hit the block and the wires suspending the drill string. The wires, immensely strong, locked off tight at the first warning, twanged like bow strings and hurled the pipes away to crash into the derrick frame. The derrick shuddered, ties broke and bent under the impact and the weight, and the whole frame buckled and crumpled into a vast honeycomb of ruin. The hose from the slush pumps was ripped open by the falling pipes. The pumps were still running and the pressure whipped the hose up and out through the debris to flail about like an angry snake spouting liquid mud in wild patterns.

High on the derrick the spidermen had seen *Circe* rush out from under the rig. There had been no bump. They watched and wondered as the boat curved round training her searchlight back on the rig. Then the mine went off. Up there they realised before anyone else what was happening. The keeling over was quickly obvious from that height. There was no time to clamber down. They jumped. One made it clear into the water, a hundred and fifty feet and he lived. The other bounced once on the main deck on the way down. He was dead when he splashed into the sea.

Those who had come from below decks ran for the sides when the canting started. Someone remembered the life-rafts, kicked the slip hooks, and saw the canisters skid over the side to split in the water and puff themselves up into shapes of safety. Some men jumped at once. Others hesitated and were caught in the avalanche of gear pouring down the deck. Men were bowled over, bruised, crushed, knocked into the sea. Some helped their injured mates; some trod on them in their haste to escape. Then the derrick fell across the deck and the ringing, clanging, screeching sound overcame the sirens, and the spurting mud splashed and gurgled and oozed over everything.

The cook in the galley felt the shudder and heard the thump of the mine. The lights flickered but stayed on, the red pilot lamps on his stove still glowed. Nothing serious. He dipped his ladle and blew into it to cool the soup for tasting. Then the cauldron slid across the stove. He put both hands on it to hold it. He pulled them back, scorched. The huge pot slid again. He realised the deck was angling under his feet. Suddenly terrified, he turned for the door but the cauldron slid, jumped, struck him, flattened him and he died there in a wave of scalding broth.

The radio man liked instructions. He waited through the explosion till his chair started swinging with the slanting deck. Fear knotted his stomach but he strained to hold his seat round against the desk and snapped the switches on the R/T to the distress frequency. "Mayday—Mayday— Mayday. Oil rig Offshore Five—Oil rig Offshore Five. We've blown up. We're going over. Mayday—Mayday— . . . . ." The deck house quivered as something struck it. He went on calling, his voice wild with fear, hoarse and high-pitched through his parched mouth. The house shuddered again and the set ripped off the bulkhead and slid towards him. He let the chair spin round. He was holding himself in it and he realised he was looking down. Down through the door which was now open and below him. There was water down there. It was like dropping through a trap-door. He let go of the chair and tumbled down through the doorway and head over heels across the deck outside into the sea.

Brad Tucker had six of the handles of the inner door free when the mine struck. He stopped for a second, feeling the shudders and sensing the explosion. He shouted for Colney, bellowing to make himself heard above the sirens. He pulled the other handles. Seven—eight—nine—ten. He tugged hard and the door flew open, throwing him back

35

against the bulkhead. He saw then that the rig was leaning over. He pulled himself through the doorway. The outer door. Ten more levers. He struck at them with his fist. One—two—three—four. The deck under his feet was already steep. He held on with one hand. Five—six— seven. He could feel things battering the shell of the hut. Eight—nine. Christ Almighty. All the levers are shut again. The angle. That's it. Gravity's swinging them shut as soon as I open them. Have to hold each one. Jam them somehow. No go. Can't hold on. He let go and found he was standing up. Standing up on what had been an upright bulkhead. Jesus. He gripped the rim of the inner door and pulled himself through. Books, bottles, instruments, everything was cascading off shelves, out of lockers, down along benches. He saw Colney, white faced, big eyed, stretched out across a bench holding himself down on top of the core sample. Tucker grabbed for the edge of a bench, the rig lurched, he missed his hold and dived at full stretch down into the wreckage of the lab.

The sirens were still screaming.

Circe came astern quickly under full power. Ellam held fiercely to the levers and watched the keeling rig. He saw things dropping into the water; men or gear, he could not tell. He saw a silver shape rearing up out of the sea in the beam of the light. A life-raft. Someone had kept his head. He heard the bleeping of the R/T in the wheelhouse and shouted to the helmsman to switch it on. "Mayday— Mayday. Oil rig Offshore Five . . . ." There was urgency and terror in every syllable. Then he heard the fearful discord of rending steel and saw the great derrick fold and collapse like a matchstick tower. The derrick would not now crash across his ship. He jerked the controls to Stop. The R/T was silent.

Johnny heard himself shouting orders to the bosun. Nets. Lifelines. Boathooks. Lights. He set the engines to Half Ahead and conned *Circe* round to head in to the doomed rig. He had both bridge searchlights on, trained ahead to pick out men in the water. The rig's main platform was almost upright, already dipping one edge into the water. The other two legs were visible, wrenched from the sea bed and buckling under the strain. The sirens wailed on like frantic women mourning their dead. Nothing was sudden. The disintegration of Offshore Five was gradual; it was like a film in slow motion. Johnny switched his eyes from the sea to the rig, to the sea, and unwillingly back to the rig. The slow subsidence went on. He saw dark fantastic shapes weaving across the wreck like infant's scribbling on a picture book. It was the mud hose but he was not to know.

Stop Engines. Near enough. Can't risk it too close. I'm their only hope. Shouting; men in the water. Dead Slow Ahead. Turn her round to starboard. Easy does it. Don't run them down. Three of them. Thank God some are alive. Stop Engines. Let her drift up to them.

He leaned over the rail, shouting to the crew. The men were alongside. Two of them had lifejackets, the red survival lights glowing. The crew had hold of them and were pulling them over the gunwale aft. One of the men was screaming. Easy, lads. They'll be hurt.

Slow Ahead again. Swing the searchlights. Keep a lookout. Something on the port bow. No, an oil drum. Something else. Stop Engines. It's a man, spreadeagled in the water, face down, still. Dead but pick him up anyway. Over there. A group of men, waving and splashing. Dead Slow Ahead. Bring her round to port. Steady her up. Stop again. Suddenly there were new sounds, loud. Shouting, splashing, gurgling, the thud of engines, creaking metal, moans, cries, the whirring of the wheel. They were loud and clear because something was missing. The sirens had stopped.

Ellam looked round. Offshore Five was almost gone. One side of the main platform jutted up out of the water, buckled legs trailing from its corners. White lights still shone from portholes, red lights still glowed round the edge

37

of the platform. The dark sea frothed and gurgled greedily as it slowly swallowed the last morsel of its prey. Johnny swung one of the searchlights on to the wreck. There were four men up there on the edge of the deck. He grabbed the loud-hailer. "Jump. Jump." They held back, crowding together, afraid. He bellowed again. "Jump. Jump. We'll pick you up." He counted. One. Two. Three. They splashed into the water.

He looked aft. The bosun waved. That other group was aboard. Hard-a-starboard. Engines set for a fast turn. *Circe* spun. Take her in stern first. The crew can haul them in aft. Stern on to the wreck and I'm ready for a quick getaway if the rig sinks fast. He swung the searchlight. Yes, three in the water. Where's the fourth? Up there, still crouched on the platform. "Jump, you stupid bastard." The man jumped. He hit one of the legs and his own legs were tangled in the steel lattice. He hung upside down, hopelessly trapped, out of reach, his yells of pain and rage turning to screams of terror and abuse as *Circe* picked up the other three and surged ahead, clear of the rig.

Johnny swung the searchlight away and fought down the sickness welling up inside. I can't take the chance. There must be others in the water. Can't risk the ship for one man. Couldn't reach him anyway. He tried to shut his ears to the screamed oaths as he took *Circe* round to the other side of the wreck.

Debris and men were all mixed up. Everything floating had to be examined. The number rescued grew steadily. Then, quite suddenly, Offshore Five had disappeared. Ellam watched the disturbed water smoothing out, then stared and felt his stomach tightening again. Offshore Five was gone but was still there, under the water, visible. There were lights and shadows and shapes down there. *Circe* drifted as her skipper gazed down into the water. There was swirling, then a great gasp and gurgle as air from some compartment escaped up to the surface. Then the lights were all snuffed out and all signs disappeared as the water rushed through to the generators and the switchboards.

Johnny rubbed a hand over his face. His mouth felt foul. He tried to spit but there was no saliva. Have to mark it, to told himself. The top can't be very deep. A ship could hit it. He turned away and shouted to the bosun to ready a marker buoy. They were there to hand. They used them for diving work. They put one over and went back to the search for survivors.

The white cruiser came back, alerted by the rig's Mayday call. The foam gun meant nothing now. The trawler steamed back too and another fishing boat from farther north on the Dogger. Ellam accepted all the help; the other boats accepted his orders. They spread out down tide and combed the sea, searchlights crisscrossing, flares soaring, bursting, waning, the R/T crackling with reports of success and failure. At last the four little ships huddled together and took a count. Thirty-seven picked up, five of them dead. Ellam's crew list showed forty-three. Six missing. Six men, either down there in the wreck of Offshore Five or in the sea, undetected. One he could account for; that one he had left trapped in the leg. He started checking names.

The man he had left on the bridge called him. London was on the R/T.

"Tell them I'm busy."

"You tell 'em, Skipper. They don't want to know me."

Johnny swore and handed the list to the bosun. He ran up to the bridge. "*Circe* here. What d'you want?"

"Who's that?"

"I told you. It's the *Circe*. Ellam."

"Are you the captain?"

"Yes, I'm the captain. What is this, a quiz game? Look, whoever you are, I've got work to do. Get on with it."

"Bright here. Roger Bright. Head Office. London."

"All right, now we're introduced. What d'you want?"

"I want to know what's happened."

Ellam was angry. "Christ Almighty, is that all? My deck's swimming in blood and guts and all you want is a report." The other voice crackled angrily. Johnny drew breath. "All right, all right, here it is. A bloody great mine blew a leg off Offshore Five. She's a wreck, sunk, kaput. I've got five bodies and thirty-two more or less alive. There's another six still missing."

"Six? Thirty-two and five's thirty-seven and six is forty-three. What about the others?"

"What others? I've got a crew list. I only put them on board a couple of days ago. I should know. Forty-three."

There was nothing from London for a few seconds. "What about Colney?"

"Who?"

"Colney, the geologist."

"God, I forgot about him. Of course, he never goes ashore. He's not on the list."

"And Tucker?"

Johnny gasped. Brad Tucker, that great, tough, warm hearted, hard living Texan, his mate on more than one night out. His voice was subdued when at last he spoke. "I forgot Brad too. That makes eight missing."

"Have you checked the survivors yet?"

"Doing it now."

"Maybe they're among them."

"Maybe. Hold on. I'll check." Ellam ran down aft. No, the bosun was sure. Yes, they had checked the survivors on the other boats. Colney and Tucker were both missing. Johnny went slowly back up to the bridge and told London.

"You're sure?" asked Bright.

"Of course I'm bloody well sure."

"Ellam, listen. Could they still be in the rig?"

"Could be. Probably are. But if they are, they're dead."

"No, they might not be. They might be trapped down there."

"They might be but it's not likely they're still alive. Anyway, what can I do? That's a big brute of a rig. I can't haul it back up on a heaving line."

"I'm going to the base now. Can you stay out there, mark the position?"

"It's marked but I'm staying out anyway. Have to warn off ships."

"Good man. I'll send the other boat out to relieve you."

"You'll be lucky. Her engine's in bits."

"Damn. Well, you'll just have to stay on. I'm coming out in a helicopter. Say about four, five hours from now."

"It'll still be dark. You can't bring a chopper out here at night."

"You let me worry about that. What about the men you picked up?"

"There are three other boats here now. I'll send them back to Yarmouth on them. They should be in by daylight. They'll need ambulances. Coffins too."

"I'll fix it. Look, Ellam, have you got diving gear on board?"

"There's a frogman. That's all."

"O.K. I'll bring what I can. Be there in a few hours. Best of luck." The set went dead.

Johnny stared at it. It's you who'll need the luck, mate, if you're going to try and land on this boat from a chopper in the middle of the night. He went out and leaned on the rail. He lit a cigarette. The smoke tasted sour in his mouth. He looked out across the water. It seemed impossible that everything should be so peaceful so soon after the disaster. It was as if it had never really happened. But it had happened and Brad Tucker was somewhere in that sea, maybe still in that rig he thought of as his own. But dead for sure.

Then his mouth fell open as he remembered the man on the leg. It couldn't be. He closed his eyes and tried to

remember. Yes, it had sounded like an American voice'
roaring abuse then screaming. There were other Americans
on Offshore Five. The two toolpushers were American. But it might have been Tucker. These three who
jumped; must check with them. God's truth. Did I
leave Brad hanging upside down to drown like an unloved
tomcat?

Chapter 4

Colney was dazed but the silenced sirens brought him to. He was lying on his back, the wreckage of his laboratory under and around him. He blinked at the lights and tried to orientate himself. He raised his head and looked around. Close to, everything was out of focus but he could see the other end of the lab clearly. He felt for his glasses. They had come off. They were somewhere amid the debris. He still clutched a piece of the core in one hand.

He sat up and peered about him. It all came back to him. The sirens then some kind of impact. Tucker rushing for the door, shouting. Then the floor heaving. He had tried to save what he could. He had flung himself across the bench to save that precious core. Then the whole hut seemed to stand on end and he was flung off the bench. It must have been some kind of explosion. Or something hitting the rig. The lab was still moving. He watched his storm coat angling on a hook on the bulkhead. Outside he could hear sounds of destruction. The inner door was swinging on its hinges, open. Tucker must have gone. I'd better go and see what happened. What a mess this place is in. I'll have to waste hours clearing it up. Just hope nothing important's been damaged. He got to his knees and started crawling towards the door. The benches gave handholds. They were still in position. They were bolted to the floor. Then the lights went out.

An ancient terror gripped him. He had always been afraid of the dark. As a child he had always slept with a nightlight in his bedroom. He hated the countryside at

43

night for there were no street lights. He realised suddenly that that was why this lab had no windows or portholes, just fluorescent tubes which burned day and night. He had explained his odd request by pointing out how unreliable daylight was, changing intensity with cloud and mist and rain. He had to have constant light for his work. That was it, constant light. He had to have artificial light because with it there was no night and therefore no terror. Till now.

He could hear his heart beating. The emergency set. He had had it all these months and never had to use it. It was in that locker near his bunk. Where was his bunk? He had lost all sense of direction. Any light would do. A torch. There was a torch on the bulkhead near the door. Is it still there? Has it fallen off and rolled away with everything else? He pulled himself up on to the end of the bench and stretched out a hand. There's the door. Feel around. No. No. Come on, torch. Where are you? Ah, there. He grasped the metal barrel and lifted it down, fumbling for the switch. Relief swept over him as the beam stabbed the darkness. The hut was moving again but there were fewer sounds outside. He swung the torch round on to the dangling coat. Good. It's swinging back upright. The floor's almost level again. Wonder what happened? Must be like that time in the Gulf when some fool started the hydraulics on one of the legs. The whole rig canted over that time. Not as badly as this. That must be it though. What about that bump? It was like an explosion. That's possible. An explosion in one of the jack compartments. Might have stripped some gearing, let the platform slip down one leg. They seem to have fixed it now. That's why the sirens have stopped. I'd better go out and see what's going on, see how long till they get the lights fixed. Damned nuisance. Just when I wanted to get on with that sample.

He hauled himself through the door to the vestibule section and shone the torch on the outer door. He could not focus properly at that short range without his glasses. He felt the water on his fingers as he fumbled for the handles. He told himself it must be rain seeping in. Tucker. That's it. Tucker didn't close the door properly when he left. Great oaf. He grasped one of the lever handles and swung it free. He had five handles off when he heard it. Then he felt it. The hiss then the jet of cold water spraying on to him. He dropped the torch and fell back from the door. He picked up the torch and shone it again on the door. The beam shuddered with the shaking of his hand. He peered, swaying to and fro, trying to focus. There was water squirting through at one edge of the door. He reached for the handles and pulled them all tight shut. The squirting and sizzling stopped. Oh, my God. He leaned over and pressed his ear to the door. What he heard was water. There were other sounds but they were muted, muffled by the water.

Colney crouched down, staring at the door. I was wrong. All wrong. Whatever it was didn't just damage the rig. It sunk it. I'm God knows how far under the sea. That change of angle, that levelling off; that was it hitting the bottom and settling down. I'm alone. I'm going to die here, slowly, as the air's used up. I'm going to poison myself with my own exhaled breath. Now they'll never know that I was right and they were wrong. All that work, all these months, all lost. All that I lived for and now no one will ever know. Everything else I've done has been a mess. Research, the university, Carol, the children. Now this, the one thing that might have made them proud of me. Damn. I'll still do it. I'll fix that emergency light and I'll write it all down. Someday, someone may find it. Even if they don't, I'll have done it. It'll be mine. The prospect of death had never worried him. It was one thing that held no terrors. In a way he welcomed it. It would solve a lot of problems. But first he had to write it all down. He scrambled back through into the laboratory.

The voice startled him.

"Limey. Limey, goddam you. Are you there?"

Colney swung the torch round the hut. He was sure it had come from inside. Tucker had not escaped. "Where are you?"

"How the hell do I know where I am?"

The torch beam picked out an arm sticking up through the mass of books and equipment piled at one end of the hut. Then Tucker's head. "I see you. I'm coming."

Brad growled.

Colney clambered along and started pulling aside the debris round the Texan. "I thought I was alone. I thought you'd got out."

"I would've been but for these crazy doors of yours. Something must've knocked me out. What the hell happened, d'you know?"

"Some sort of explosion I suppose."

"I'd guessed that much." He stifled a cry. "Take it easy, will you. My leg hurts."

"Sorry," said Colney and went on excavating. Tucker's left leg was pinned under a gas cylinder which had broken loose and crashed the whole length of the hut. The geologist lifted it clear. "How does that feel?"

Tucker moved the leg and clenched his teeth against the pain. "It don't feel too good."

"I'll see what I can do. I used to do a bit of first aid."

"Never mind the first aid. Just give me a hand and help me crawl out of this place. I want to know what's going on outside."

"I'm afraid you can't go outside, Tucker."

"Quit telling me what I can't do. Just give me a hand, will you. I'll make it."

Colney's voice was quiet and controlled. "The rig's sunk, Tucker. I calculate that we're about eighty or ninety feet under water."

"You're joking, man. So where's all the water?"

"It's outside. We're sealed off in here. I tried the outside door. The water was spurting in as soon as I started to swing the handles free."

Tucker said nothing for fully a minute. "Sure is quiet. I guess you're right." His voice had lost its aggressiveness. "It must've been some explosion to sink old Offshore Five. She's been through some pretty rough weather. Maybe some ship hit us."

"Maybe. Anyway we're here. I'll just get my glasses and fix a light, then I'll look at your leg." He found his spare glasses in a drawer in one of the benches and delved down into the wreckage to the locker where the emergency lighting set was kept. His fingers fumbled with the wires. He realised that the hut was getting cold. He shivered. He pressed the switch and the bulb lit up. After the darkness, even the single shaded bulb seemed immensely bright. "That's better." He rubbed his hands together to warm them. "It's a bit chilly. Just hold on for a minute while I get a jacket or something."

"I'm not likely to run away," said Brad.

Colney went over and took his padded anorak off the hook on the bulkhead. He put it on and came back to where the Texan was lying. "Now let's have a look at that leg of yours."

Brad eased himself up till he was lying almost flat on top of the debris. He watched as Colney slit through his oilskin trousers and denims with a pocket-knife. He gritted his teeth as the pain came. Colney pulled the two legs gently together. "How's it look?" asked Brad.

"Not too bad. I'll need your belt." He unclipped the big leather belt and pulled it clear. He slipped it under Tucker's thighs just above the knee and pulled it tight, then down and round his ankles. "That should do. Now I'd better find that first aid box."

"In this mess? You'll be lucky."

"No, it shouldn't be too difficult. Let me see. It was in that locker over there. The locker's empty now but, with the way the deck angled, if something fell from that locker, it should be somewhere over in that corner." He crawled over and searched around with the torch. He was back in a couple of minutes. "There you are. Just simple geometry."

Brad shook his head as the geologist opened the box and started work on the leg. "You're a cool one, Limey."

"Why's that?"

Tucker laughed. " 'Why's that?' he says. We're sunk ninety feet down under the North Sea and you think that finding a first-aid kit's just simple geometry. D'you know something? You haven't said or done anything as if you're scared since you found me. Are you so sure they'll find us and get us out?"

"Get us out?"

"Yes, get us out. Or isn't that just simple geometry?"

"Keep still a moment. This may hurt." He worked in silence for a bit. "To be honest, Tucker, it had never occurred to me that we could get out."

Brad gaped. "You must be nuts. Of course they can get us out. They get men out of submarines, don't they. They'll get us out. It's only a matter of time."

"Is it? Yes, I suppose it is. How does that feel? I've immobilised the leg." He was glad Tucker was not asking questions about that leg. It had a horrible compound fracture, the bone shattered and poking out through the flesh. He had done what he could but that was not much.

"It's fine. I don't feel too much. Thanks." He propped himself up on one elbow. "I don't get you. Aren't you interested in getting out of here?" He pulled a cigar from his pocket, peeled off the wrapping with his teeth, and flipped it up into his mouth.

"You'd better not smoke. No, it's not so much that I object. It's just that this is all the air we'll have till they find us. As you say, it's probably only a matter of time. But we don't know how long."

Brad took the cigar out of his mouth and licked his lips.

"You don't have to put it away. Just don't light it. They say it's just as good sucking it unlit. It's all psychological, you know. It's just an adult substitute for breast feeding or thumb sucking."

"You don't say," said the Texan slowly. "Now if you're finished curing my cigar habit, will you answer my question? Are you interested in getting out of here?"

Colney sat down and leaned back against one of the benches. "Terrible mess in here. I'll have to start clearing up." He rubbed his jaw. "Yes, I suppose I am, now. I wasn't before I found you. I just assumed I was going to die. It never occurred to me that I could be rescued. It seems different now there are two of us. It's funny that should make any difference. But it does. I was really quite annoyed when you called out. I had sort of accepted it by then. I'd decided what to do. It all seemed quite simple."

Brad had forgotten to put the cigar back in his mouth "I'm sorry I gatecrashed your little party."

"That's all right. As I say, it seems different now. I suppose we will be rescued. I suppose we should plan for that. Even if we're not, it won't be the same. Not with two of us, and you with a broken leg."

"What the hell's my busted leg got to do with it?"

"Well, you know how it is with injured people. You feel compelled to help them, to change your plans, to consider them first, even though when they're in one piece you wouldn't say Good Morning to them. Nothing personal, of course, Tucker. It's just that it's not so simple and straightforward any more."

"Don't mind me. I'm pretty thick-skinned." He put the cigar into his mouth and chewed on the end. "Tell me, Limey, what was it you'd decided to do before I got in the way?"

Colney smiled wanly. "You wouldn't be interested."

"Try me."

"I was just going to finish writing up some ideas I've been working on. Pet subject of mine. I think it's pretty important. I wanted to put it all down on paper. That way I would be sure I'd done what I started to do. I suppose that doesn't make sense to you."

"It sounds sort of crazy, makes sense, both at the same time. But whatever this is, if it's so important, why don't you want to be there, up there, when people hear your ideas?"

"I thought you'd say that, Tucker. You and me, we're different, that's all. Knowledge, discovery, that's what interests me. I can't be doing with all the fuss and the flattery and the bitchiness. Scientists are a bitchy lot, you know. I don't get on very well with people."

Brad spat some chewed tobacco. "I'll say one thing for you, Limey. Sucking cigars is better than nothing at all."

They said nothing for several minutes, Colney sitting staring along into the dim part of the lab, Tucker trying to shift himself into a more comfortable position and growling now and then as the pain stabbed at him.

It was Brad who broke the silence. "How are we fixed for food?"

"Food? Oh yes, I suppose we'll have to think about that kind of thing. Let me think. I've got some chocolate somewhere. That's all."

"I've got a candy bar here."

"Wait, I never ate my supper. I took it from the man at the door and put it down somewhere. I suppose it's somewhere in all this mess."

"Any water?"

"There's plenty in the taps. Oh no, I suppose the pipes are all broken. That's funny, isn't it. Fancy dying of thirst in the middle of the North Sea. It's like that poem."

"I'm not laughing."

"Wait a minute. There's plenty of distilled water. At least there was. I'll look for it."

"There's no hurry. I was just wondering how we were fixed."

"No, I'll look. Anyway, it's pretty cold. A bit of exercise

will warm me up." He got up and started moving the debris. "You can't be very comfortable there, Tucker. I'll fix up the bunk for you." He cleared away some wreckage and straightened the mattress. It took him some time to move the big man on to the bunk. Tucker never complained but the cold sweat on his brow was proof of his agony. Colney tucked a pillow under his head and spread a blanket over him. "How's that? I'll try and find that water now."

Brad nodded.

The big jar of distilled water was intact. Its basket jacket had saved it. It was almost half full. It took longer to find something to drink from but at last Colney found a beaker still wedged in its rack. He poured some water and took it over to the Texan.

"Thanks, Colney. That's better."

The geologist took a drink himself. It tasted flat and uninteresting but it was wet. He drained the beaker and began trying to make sense of his books and equipment. The noises he made sounded hollowly in the hut. All round them was the vast insulation of the sea.

"What was that?" Tucker was up on one elbow.

"I didn't hear . . ."

"Quiet."

They waited. It seemed far off but it was distinct. Tap tap tap. Tap—Tap—Tap. Then again. Tap tap tap. They stared at each other.

"How long since we went in?" asked Brad.

Colney looked at his watch. The second hand was still moving. "Half an hour. An hour. I don't know."

"It could be them. If the workboat got clear, it could be them. There's a diver on board. Listen, man. Try and trace that tapping."

The sound came again. It seemed to come from the far end. Colney scrambled along to that end of the lab. He listened again. Yes, it was somewhere there. He pressed his ear to the bulkhead. No, not here. Farther along. He moved and listened. Nothing. He pounded on the panels with his fist. There it is again. He pounded again and got a reply and traced it downwards. He traced it till he seemed to be right over the spot. He had his ear to the deck.

"It's coming from underneath," he called to Tucker. "What's underneath?"

"Underneath? Nothing. This hut's up on a deck of its own. Here, wait a minute. If that deck's collapsed, we'll be down on the main platform, right over one of the pump-rooms."

Colney listened. The message was easily read. "It's someone else, inside the rig. He's sending SOS." He started tapping back in Morse, asking who it was. The reply was the same, but more urgent, SOS. As he lay listening, Colney wondered how a sound could be so visual. He could see it all. There was a man down there, trapped in the high part of the pump room, on the ladder maybe. Why didn't we hear him before? Maybe he was knocked out too. Now he's come round. He's alone and in the dark and frightened. The tapping was frantic now. It was just senseless hammering, even the bare three letters were indistinguishable. What was happening down there? The water, that must be it. The water must be rising down there, creeping up, forcing the trapped man higher up the ladder, compressing his prison. The banging now sounded with the full force of the man's desperation. He had reached the top of the ladder and found his way barred by steel. The water was over his ankles, his knees, his waist. There was less volume in the sound now but it was continuous. There was no space left to wield the hammer or the spanner at full stretch. Up to his chest, over his shoulders, lapping at his chin. A final flurry of tiny blows. Colney thought he heard a long, choking scream but knew it was only in his mind. He beat on the deck himself. He listened. Nothing.

He came back to where Brad was lying. "I was wrong, Tucker. It's not easy to die. When it comes, you fight it."

"Poor bastard. I wonder how many of the others got off?"

They were both silent. There was a new and terrible sense of their own danger. The lab no longer seemed a haven, keeping them safe till the rescuers arrived. Now it was like a tomb.

Tucker was the first to hear it. "Are you sure you locked off that outside door?"

"Yes. Why?"

"Listen."

Colney held his breath. It was difficult to pick up at first. It was not loud. It was like the sound of insects flocking at sunset over water. That was it. Water. That noise was water and it was slowly, stealthily, seeping into their refuge.

Chapter 5

Roger pushed down the accelerator as the de-restriction signs showed black on white in the headlights. The Thunderbird surged ahead with a well-bred roar from the exhaust. That's better. Clear of Thetford—time, half past midnight. Fifty miles to the base at Yarmouth. An hour, maybe less now the road's clear. Couldn't be slower than that first eighty miles from London. More than two hours. The first hour getting through London on to the A11 and up past Epping. What a time to choose for a do like this. Saturday night and throwing out time for the pubs. He smiled. Who am I to talk? The way I was driving everyone must have thought I was full to the gills.

He dipped for a lorry then flicked the main beams back on. There was a long straight stretch ahead. The speedometer proved the power under the bonnet. He drove with the sure light touch of the expert. His eyes were on the road but his brain was checking back on all the arrangements, double checking to find anything missed. It was not much more than three hours since that first report of Offshore Five's distress call. A lot had happened since then.

At first, just for a few seconds, he could not believe the message. He had worked on a lot of rigs in a lot of different places. None had ever blown up. There was nothing on board to blow up. There was machinery, of course, but a pump or a generator would not demolish a rig like Offshore Five. And he knew that it must have been something big enough to do that. The coast station was adamant. They could not raise the rig on the R/T. The Mayday message had been cut off half-way through. It could have been a ship. That had happened before, a ship colliding with a rig. But why say, "We've blown up"? It could have been a gas explosion in the hole. Not likely though. Time enough for all that later. Get things moving now at this end. They'll need help out there on Dogger.

There was an emergency routine. The night controller had already started it. Call Yarmouth base—recall staff and crews—make ready helicopters and workboats—break out all emergency gear—arrange liaison with coast station and other rescue groups. Roger himself had started chasing up his personal assistant, Harry Ashton, by phone. An *au pair* answered his home number. It took five frustrating minutes to discover that Harry and his wife were at the theatre. There was a quicker response there. The manager sensed the urgency, sent someone to page Harry, and had a taxi waiting at the door. Ashton was in the office in less than fifteen minutes with his wife. When she heard what the flap was, she went on home. Oilmen's wives soon learn to be long-suffering.

Roger had tried not to think of all the consequences of the disaster. He still knew no details so he concentrated on covering every chance. Yarmouth reported that the workboat *Circe* had been on station. Call the workboat. Maybe it had survived whatever had happened. Yes, it had. It was picking survivors up now. God, so it was really bad. Survivors meant that the rig was wrecked. Get me the skipper. Never mind if he's busy. Get me the skipper. That skipper, what was his name—Ellam. He sounded a pretty rough diamond but he'd done a good job getting so many off. It had been a mine. A chance in a million. Who'd have thought of a mine twenty years after the war was over. Pity Ellam didn't do such a good job spotting that mine. I'll have to find out about that. But not right away. That can wait. He's out there so he's important. No post-mortem till it's all over.

Bright changed down for a double bend then rammed the

Thunderbird back up into top. Ted Colney—he's the key man. Without him the whole plan falls apart. He's the key man so he's also the weak link. Stupid of me to rely on him so much. I should have had others working out there, checking, making sure. But that wouldn't have worked. Ted wouldn't have let anyone work with him. And no one who knew him would have taken on the job anyway. Colney's name's like a red rag to a bull with other geologists. He's got revolutionary ideas about where to find oil. The fact that he often finds it doesn't make the others like him any more. He's got to be alive. He wasn't among the survivors but he was working on that core in that special lab of his. He could still be in there. It's just like a sealed tank. He could be alive. Even if he's dead there could be notes, bits of that last core. If I can get a diver in there I might still get enough to make a decision in time for that deadline.

The glow of Norwich was ahead. Tucker—he's the other chance. He's the only other one who might know if Ted's discovered anything important. He's missing too. Not likely that he's trapped anywhere. He's the type who'd be outside on the platform at the first sign of trouble. Offshore Five was very much his rig. Damn, I should have told Ellam to question all the survivors to find out if any of them had seen Tucker or Colney. Never mind, maybe Ellam had the savvy to do it himself. If not I'll have it done as soon as they get into the base at daylight. Pity though if Tucker's dead. Offshore men like him are hard to come by. Let's not assume it's all hopeless till I get out there. At least I've covered the chance that Colney's still in the rig, alive.

He smiled as he remembered that phone call to the Navy. The duty commander already knew about the rig. He understood that ships in the area were already picking up survivors. Bright had not bothered with the exact truth, that there might still be some men trapped inside. He was definite. There were men still trapped inside—there was little time—action was needed at once. The commander wanted to be sure. How did Bright know? A frogman had been down. It worked. A frigate was going to be out there with divers and equipment the next morning. This morning, Sunday. Time enough for apologies when it was certain no one was still alive down in the rig.

Norwich. Roger took the ring road to meet the A47 for Yarmouth. He checked his watch. Much better now. Barely thirty-five minutes for the thirty miles from Thetford. What's that ahead? Looks like a police car. Slow down. Don't take a chance of being booked for speeding. Come on. Turn off, you bastards, and chase some real criminals. I'm in a hurry. That's it. Down that road back to town and let me get on my way. The police car turned off, Bright drove sedately past the end of the road, glanced left to check that the patrol car was really retreating, then stabbed the throttle hard.

Clear of Norwich he settled down for the last twenty miles to Yarmouth. The road was deserted. The base would be humming with activity now. Jack Henderson was a good manager; the kind who could fill in all the details, given broad instructions. The big helicopter would be fuelled up and loaded with all the gear Bright had asked for. Clothing would be ready for him; he had left London without even the panic bag he kept ready for sudden calls. The stuff in it would be useless out there in the North Sea. Already work would have started getting the second workboat ready for sea. Ambulances and hospital beds would be ready for the survivors coming at daylight. All the latest news from *Circe* would be there in a file ready for him. There would be weather reports, flight plans for the helicopter, instructions for homing on the workboat and drill for putting him on board. The press boys would be there but Henderson knew how to keep them happy.

Bright grinned. He had dodged the reporters in London. Harry Ashton was in charge there now; he could handle them. But some would be up at the base already or hot on his tail. The North Sea oil search was news and Roger Bright was an important part of that news. He accepted that. Newspapermen could be a nuisance but they were an important link in spreading the word. He was always polite, even friendly; he always gave them as much information as the secrecy of the oil business allowed; he was not averse to letting them fly his kites for him. He had been the answer to the newsmen's prayers. They had given him the whizz-kid treatment. Briton Heads Yankee North Sea Search. Bright By Name—Bright By Nature. Brightboy Chases Black Gold. Yes, they would be there. Dateline Yarmouth 2 a.m. Sunday. Exclusive—Disaster Stops North Sea Pacesetter. Don't be too quick with that headline, boys. I'm not stopped yet. Not by a long chalk.

He thought about that helicopter. He knew it was not easy to fly these things over the sea at night, and even more difficult to make a rendezvous with something as small as *Circe*. Thank God we've started to use the big ones. With one of the small ones I'd have been in trouble. They were one-way jobs, needing refuelling on the rig for the journey home. No rig now. But the big ones can do the round trip on one fill. He gripped the steering-wheel hard as he thought of being winched down on to the workboat. Come on, Brightboy, you'll just have to grin and bear it. It was your idea. Put on your most nonchalant face. You can't let your staff know you're scared of heights. How'd it be if they all knew you got butterflies every time you climb a ladder? How'd it be if it got out that you messed your pants that time off Texas when a craneman swung you aboard fast in one of those rope cages? That would spoil your image, Brightboy. Just hook on that harness and step out into space. Remember what it's all about. Hundreds of millions of pounds.

Yarmouth. Not yet one-thirty. The deserted streets looked damp under the cold light of the street lamps. Wisps of mist drifted across the lights. Not fog, please not fog, not now. Down to the front and along beside the high wire fence bounding the base area. The whole place was ablaze with light. He swung the car in and stopped in front of the main gates. The horns brought the guard running from his hut. Roger held up his pass against the windscreen for identification. The gates were already open and the man was waving him in. The white Thunderbird was all the pass he needed. He waved to the guard and drove through and across to the main building beside the helicopter pad. One of the big planes was out there on the pad with a fuel truck alongside.

Henderson was in the doorway of the office and came running out as the car squealed to a halt. "You made pretty good time, Mr. Bright."

Roger got out and stretched himself. "Not too bad, Jack. Slow through London but the rest of the way was fairly fast. Anything new?"

"Not much. It's all ready for you inside. It's a bad business."

"You can say that again. We'll have to chase these shipyards now. With Offshore Five gone, these new rigs are absolutely essential."

The warmth struck them as they came into the building. Henderson looked at his chief. "That's true. But I meant it was a bad business about the men on Five. Thirteen dead or missing and God knows how many of the others may die yet."

"Yes, it's a bad show. Let's hope some of them are still alive down in the rig."

"In here." They went into the conference room. Henderson poured coffee. "That's what you're hoping, of course, going out there at night in a chopper. It'll be that crazy geologist you're worried about."

"Ted Colney's not so crazy, Jack. He's a bit odd but he knows what he's doing with rocks." Bright sipped the scalding coffee. "That's better." He lit a cigarette. "But you're right, I'm worried about him. We had better find him alive down there. If we don't, this whole drilling programme will be a write-off." He drank some more coffee. "Let's see what you've got, Jack."

The manager lifted a file from the table and handed it over. "There's not much you won't know already." He watched as Bright went through the papers. He admired Roger. He admired him for his youth, his drive, his efficiency. But it was a grudging admiration for he could never understand his callousness about people. When he was organising, they were numbers on his charts. They had no names, no flesh and blood, no feelings. They were units to use and discard as it suited. That was one Roger Bright; the real one, Henderson suspected. There was another Roger Bright. The public face. Then he could joke, make men laugh, win them over, remember their first names, where they had worked before, recall unimportant details about their background and their interests. This was the Roger Bright most people knew, especially the press men. I'd better tell him about the press men. He'd never forgive me if I forgot.

"All very thorough as usual, Jack." Bright handed back the file. "The weather seems all right. No beefs from the chopper pilot?"

"Not this one. It's Macandrew. D'you know him? He's game for anything."

"Macandrew. Yes, I know him. Red haired, lovely Highland voice, freckles, and a huge capacity for Scotch."

"That's him. He's got it all worked out with Johnny Ellam. They talked on the R/T."

Roger was stripping off his clothes. "That's one I don't know, Jack. Ellam, I mean. I talked to him to-night. Seemed a bit rough but knows what he's doing. Is that right?"

"He's a hard case, all right. But you're lucky you've got him out there. He's a Geordie. Not very strong on etiquette but he's right on top of his job."

"Sounds useful." Bright was into the nylon coveralls and was starting to don the lined survival suit.

"The Press is here, by the way. What'll I do? Give them another drink and tell them there's nothing new?"

"No, Jack, send them in. I'll talk to them while I'm dressing. It'll save money on the booze."

Henderson walked across the room. Send them in. That was predictable. Send them in. Switch on the public face. A few quick quotes. Hold that pose with hand on zip. Caption—Boss Flies To Rescue. He opened the door and called the reporters. It's all in a good cause. Thirteen dead or missing.

The reporters came in, tired eyed but full of questions.

"Mr. Bright, how bad is it out there?"

"How's this going to affect your plans in the North Sea?"

"What's the latest count on dead and missing?"

"Can we have the names?"

"You're going out there, Mr. Bright. What do you expect to be able to do?"

Roger held up his hand for silence. He fixed his Mae West and Henderson started strapping on the winch harness. "Gentlemen, please. I can only tell you what I know. That is that our rig, Offshore Five, has been destroyed by a floating mine. Thirteen of the crew of forty-five are either dead or missing. The survivors are due in here at the base about daylight. We're sure that some of the men are still in the rig, trapped down there underwater. That's why I'm going out now in a helicopter. I'm going to be winched down on to our workboat, *Circe*, which did a great job saving so many of the crew and is still standing by out there. The Navy's coming out with divers to try and save the men who are trapped. That's all there is, boys."

"What about some details, Mr. Bright. Can we have the names of the dead and missing, addresses of their next of kin, anything about this mine?"

"Jack Henderson here will give you everything you need just as soon as it's available."

"Just one more question."

"Go ahead."

"Mr. Bright, you're the boss of this company. Why are you going out in a helicopter in the middle of the night? Isn't that pretty dangerous? Couldn't someone else go?"

"That sounded like three questions. But the answer's simple." He looked down for a moment then up, directly at the newsmen. "Yes, I'm the boss. But these men out there, trapped down in that rig, they're part of this company too. I know them. I've worked with them. They're my friends. I want them out of that wreck, alive. That's why I'm going."

The reporters nodded and scribbled in their note-books.

Henderson pulled the harness buckle tight. He felt rather sick. "That helicopter's waiting," he said.

"Thanks, Jack." He started for the door. "Good-bye, boys."

"Good luck, Mr. Bright."

In the corridor a young man called to them. "Mr. Henderson, is this the Mr. Bright who's flying out to the rig?"

"I'm Bright. What is it?"

"This is the Immigration Officer," explained Henderson.

"How do you do. You'll excuse me. I'm in a bit of a rush."

"I just wanted to check your passport, sir."

Roger stared at him. "I'm not in the mood for jokes."

"I assure you it's not a joke, sir. Anyone flying off outside the three mile limit must go through a passport check."

"That is the rule," said Henderson.

"I know the rule, Jack," snapped Bright. "I sat on the committee that worked out the rules. This is an emergency. I'm not going out to the rig. There is no rig."

"I must insist, sir."

"You can insist as much as you like. My passport's in London. You're not going to see it. I'm taking off in that helicopter. And you're not going to stop me."

The young man was flustered. "Rules are rules, Mr. Bright. You can't take off."

Bright put a hand on the man's shoulder. His voice was quiet. "Behind that door there are four newspapermen. Would you like me to tell them about this? They're desperate for a good headline." He turned away and started for the main entrance. "Come on, Jack."

Outside, the two men walked across the pad to the waiting plane. The huge blades started whirling and the engine noise shattered the night air. Bright's shouted good-bye was lost in the din. He clambered up into the plane and took the seat beside the pilot. Macandrew nodded to him and handed over a headset with padded earphones and a microphone. Roger put it on and the noise receded.

"Good evening, ladies and gentlemen. This is Captain Macandrew. Welcome aboard this Inoco aircraft, Apple Delta. In a few minutes we will be taking off for an unknown destination far out in the . . ."

"Get on with it, man," growled Bright.

The pilot chuckled. "Apple Delta to base tower. Am I clear to lift off?"

"You're clear, Apple Delta."

The rotors screamed and the noise penetrated through the earpieces. The plane shuddered and Roger saw the lighted pad starting to recede. The nose dipped sharply as Macandrew trimmed the aircraft. Roger's stomach contracted. Then they were clear, over the harbour, heading out over the dark water, the lights of the base getting smaller and falling astern.

"How long will it take you?"

"About an hour," said Macandrew. "If we have no trouble finding her, that is."

"Do you expect any?"

"Can't tell. Weather's all right just now. I'll call them up when I think I'm fifty miles off. If it's still clear they'll be able to mark themselves with a searchlight."

"And if it's not clear?"

"Then we'll try homing on a radio signal. If that doesn't work, we'll go back home to base."

"Let's just assume we're going to find them. What's the drill for lowering me and all this gear?"

"There's nothing to it. It's just like playing Peter Pan. The wire hardly ever breaks, you know." The Scotsman's voice was bubbling with humour.

Bright bit back the sharp reply that was on his lips. "That's encouraging," he said. "What's the actual drill?"

Macandrew explained it carefully. All the stores had been loaded ready slung. They would hook on a load, toss it out, and Macandrew would lower away on the winch. He would be in touch with Ellam all the time on the R/T so he would know how to handle the plane to drop each load plumb on to the deck. After all the cargo was gone, it would be Roger's turn. All very simple barring high winds, a big sea, winch or wire failure, the lights on *Circe* going out, or the chopper's engines packing up. Bright nodded his way through the explanation then sat staring out into the darkness. The pilot's flippancy was beginning to annoy him.

Now and again a ship's wake showed white on the water far below. Sixty miles out they spotted three wakes in line ahead heading for Yarmouth. The two trawlers and the cruiser were on their way in with the survivors. Macandrew called them up for news. They had nothing to add to what Roger already knew. The surface wind was Force 2, hardly any sea. Good conditions for getting down on to the workboat. Five minutes later the pilot started calling *Circe*.

"Apple Delta calling *Circe*. Apple Delta calling *Circe*. Do you read me?"

"I read you, you big red-haired heathen. Where've you been?"

"Hallo, Johnny boy. I'm taking it easy. I've got a VIP aboard. Show me a light, will you."

"Coming up."

Up ahead and a bit to the left twin shafts of light sprang out from the darkness.

"Got you, Johnny. About twenty-five minutes."

"We're ready when you are, Mac."

The plane had the searchlight beams dead ahead now. They flew on, not talking. Macandrew was concentrating on flying the plane, Roger was thinking about that descent. He knew it was just one of these things he would do. When the stakes were big enough, there was very little that would stop Roger Bright. But it was a long twenty-five minutes.

The beams grew brighter and bigger and moved closer under the nose of the plane. Suddenly there were more lights and they were almost over the ship. *Circe*'s shape was etched in deck lights. From up there it looked a minute target.

Roger thanked Macandrew, took off his headset and moved back into the plane to hook on the cargo. He watched each load down, swinging on the end of the wire, lowering, stopping, steadying, then dropping the last few feet on to the deck. One load missed the deck and plunged into the sea, to appear again as the pilot hauled it up, steadied, then landed it on the boat. Without earphones, Roger was saved from Ellam's and Macandrew's witticisms about trying that trick with the boss.

At last the loads were gone. The pilot waved Bright forward and hooked the wire on to his harness. Roger walked back to the open door and squatted down on the floor with his legs hanging over the edge. He looked up. The wire was tight through the block. Macandrew was grinning and pointing down. Roger leaned out and felt the downward thrust of the slipstream on his head and shoulders. He sat there, gripping the edge of the floor with his fingers, breathing deeply. Suddenly the plane canted over and he slipped off into space.

Chapter 6

Down on the workboat, Johnny Ellam watched from the wing of the bridge. A trailing lead ran back to the R/T set in the wheelhouse. Macandrew was in high spirits.

"Our VIP's a reluctant VIP, Johnny. He doesn't want to jump. He's sitting back there on the edge like a two year old who's scared of the water."

"Give him time, Mac. I don't know I'd like to jump myself."

"I can't hang around up here. I'll help him on his way."

"Take it easy," barked Ellam but as he said it he saw the helicopter heel over and the silver suited figure appear suddenly in the searchlights.

"There you are," came the Highland voice. "Quite painless. Winching down now."

Johnny watched the slow descent. The downdraught from the plane stirred his hair and drew rucked patterns on the water all around. It had been a long wait, out there all alone, keeping station on Offshore Five's grave, wondering if Brad Tucker was still down there, and if he was still alive. He could be; that much was certain. It wasn't Brad who got caught in that leg. Ellam had checked with all the survivors before the boats left. It had been one of the toolpushers who had jumped and not made it. No one was sure about Tucker but he had last been seen going into the geology hut. When the boats left, Johnny took *Circe* round and round looking for anyone in the water who had been missed. There was no one. A few pieces of wreckage but not much of that. The weather was good.

He let the boat drift, then brought her back on station, drift again, then back to where she started. Lookouts were posted to spot ships passing dangerously close. The radar scanned continuously but nothing came to disturb the grim peacefulness. The coast stations were warning all ships to keep clear of the area.

He had talked to base to fix procedure for the rendezvous with the helicopter, then he left the bosun on the bridge and went below to his cabin to try and rest. He dozed off but his sleep was fitful. That mine floated through his dreams. Where had it come from? Why didn't I spot it sooner? Was I wrong chasing that white boat? Why'd the rig's radar not picked up the mine? That one's easy. They switch it off when the boat's patrolling. What would have happened if I'd done nothing? Maybe it would have floated through and clear away downtide. Odds are it would. So I blew up Offshore Five. I killed and mangled all those men. I trapped Brad down there. Maybe I killed him too. So it went on, round and round in his brain as he tossed and turned on his bunk, coming half awake, losing the terror with the familiar sight of his cabin, then slipping back into sleep and doubt. The bosun called him after two. The chopper was on its way.

Now there it was, up above, Macandrew chatting away, and this man Bright dangling on the end of the wire.

"You're very quiet, Johnny. Anything wrong? Has he fallen off the end?"

"He's still there. Why don't you shut up for a minute and get him down?"

"Keep your wool on then."

"Sorry, Mac." He watched, judging angles and distance. "Hold it there." He gave *Circe* a touch of engines and rudder to swing her stern round under the man on the wire. "That's it. Lower away easy." The figure dropped down to a few feet above the deck. "Hold it." Men ran across the deck and grasped the dangling legs. "O.K. We've got him. Slack right down." The wire ran and

Bright was on board. "Very neat. He's unhooked. You can go back to bed now, you lucky man."

The headphones crackled with an Al Jolson tune. "Oh Great Yarmouth, here I come. Right back where I started from."

Ellam grinned and pulled off the headset. Macandrew took life even less seriously than he did. That was saying something. The noise of the plane was already receding.

He watched the men on deck stripping off Bright's Mae West and harness. So now I'm to meet the great Roger Bright in person. Never heard of him till a few hours ago. I wonder how that was? The bosun says everyone knows Roger Bright. Haven't you heard the stories? Don't you read the papers, Skipper? Of course I don't read the papers. What sailors read papers? There's no delivery at sea. No, I do read the papers when I'm ashore. The sports pages and the strip cartoons. And the juicy bits. What else is there? A whizz-kid, eh. I don't trust him. Hold it, that's going too far. Remember Captain Bruce of the *Monarch*. There was a whizz-kid. I got to like him a lot. And this one's pretty quick too. He's the one who thought there might be men still alive down there.

Roger was waddling up the ladder to the bridge, awkward in his survival suit. At the top he held out his hand. "You'll be Johnny Ellam. Glad to meet you. I'm Bright."

"That's more than I am at this time in the morning."

Roger smiled. "Maybe a little bit corny but not bad for openers."

Johnny grinned. He was already seeing the Brightboy magic. "You'd better come below and get that fancy suit off. You don't look comfortable."

"Where's the rig? Is there anything to see?"

Ellam swung the searchlight down and across the water. This one doesn't waste any time. "That's all there is." The beam picked out the fluttering flag on the staff of the marker buoy.

"Well, at least we know where it is. Let's go below."

Down in his cabin Ellam shouted for coffee and helped Bright out of his survival suit. As he stripped, Roger looked round the room. Johnny watched him. It's like that Kim's Game the Scouts used to play. I'll bet in another minute he'll be able to list everything in the cabin. He's sharp, this one. I'll have to watch it. Sharp types usually finish up pricking me.

"It's small in here but comfortable," said Roger. "Are you happy with this job?"

"It's a change. I was happy till a few hours ago."

"You did a fine job, Johnny. Now let's get together and try and finish it off." He took the mug of coffee from the cook. "Smells wonderful." He sipped at it. "Tastes wonderful too. Now, Johnny, I want you to show me exactly what happened. I brought a plan of Offshore Five with me."

They cleared the desk and spread the plan. Ellam pointed. "That's the leg the mine hit. That one at the apex. Nothing seemed to happen for a bit. Only seconds, I suppose. Then the whole bloody thing keeled over." He tried to illustrate it with his hands. "I'd sounded the alarm. They heard it for all the sirens on the rig started sounding off. I suppose that's why most of them got up on deck in time. Then the derrick collapsed. It fell back right across the platform."

"Wait a minute. If the derrick collapsed back across the platform, then it must have fallen right on top of the geology hut. That's here, isn't it."

"That's right. Hadn't thought of that. It probably did. Almost certain."

"So if there's anyone in that hut we'll have to clear away all the wreckage of the derrick first to get at them."

"I guess so."

"Damn." Roger drummed on the desk with his fingers. "Never mind. That's assumption. Let's find out what it's really like down there. Get that frogman of yours, Johnny."

"D'you want him now? I told him to turn in. I knew you'd want him at daylight. I thought he should get some sleep."

"Daylight? I want him now."

"What for? We can get everything ready. It'll only take minutes to brief him. He might as well get what rest he can."

"Johnny, if anyone's alive down there I want him found. I'm not waiting for daylight. That'll be hours yet. When is sunrise out here?"

"About seven just now. That's only three hours. It's dangerous diving in the dark. And anyway, he's done his time."

"What does that mean?"

"He did half an hour on the legs yesterday. He can't dive for sixteen hours after that. Unless you want to kill him."

"When did he dive yesterday?"

"He finished between noon and one."

"So this sixteen hours will be up in less than an hour."

"Even so you can't ask him to dive till it's light."

"I'm going to. I didn't bring all that gear out here just for fun. Are you going to call that frogman, Ellam?"

Johnny turned round and buzzed the bridge. Just what I thought. The pricking's started already. When the bridge answered he told the man he wanted the diver rousted out. He hooked up the phone, slumped into a chair and lit a cigarette.

Bright looked up from the plan of the rig. "What's the depth of water here?"

"About fifteen fathoms. That's ninety feet to shore-wallahs."

"I see. So, depending how the rig settled, the geology hut could be anything from about seventy to ninety feet down. Is that right?"

"What's it matter? You'll find out soon enough."

Roger pulled over the other chair and sat down facing

Ellam. "All right, Johnny. I know there are dangers in diving in the dark. But let's ask the diver what he thinks."

"You don't have to worry about him. Bert Thomas will dive anytime, anywhere. Don't ask him. Tell him. He was trained in the Marines. All he needs is an order."

"That's a useful asset."

"It can be deadly."

"Delay could be deadly too," snapped Bright. "If anyone's still down there, every minute's precious. The air's being used up, maybe water's coming in. By daylight maybe no one will be left alive. Have you thought of that?"

"Of course I have. What can we do? Bert can dive, maybe contact someone trapped, they can tap messages to each other, but that's as far as we can go." He sucked on his cigarette. "Why take risks when all that can happen is that some poor bastard thinks he's saved then has to go back to dying slowly?"

"I'm not playing games, Johnny. There's a Navy frigate on its way here now with divers and special equipment. I want to know if anyone's down there so that frigate can have everything ready for action the minute it arrives."

"That's my point. You're risking Thomas's life in a night dive to save a few minutes when the Navy gets here."

Roger nodded. "That's right. It only takes three minutes to die by drowning or suffocation."

"Have it your own way, Mr. Bright. But don't dress it up for my benefit. You're not in a hurry just because you want to save anyone. You're in a hurry because you want to know if that crazy geologist's alive down there. You've only talked about that hut. There are eight missing. They're not all in there. I suppose you have your reasons. Here's Bert now."

Ellam introduced the diver. Roger began explaining what he wanted done. When he finished he asked Thomas if he was prepared to try it at night. The diver was surprised to be asked. He wanted to do it. He wanted to try out the new equipment Roger had brought with him. Johnny

71

was pleased too. He wanted desperately to know if Brad Tucker was still alive. The three of them went down on to the deck to get things ready.

It was almost five o'clock when Thomas was ready to go. He was festooned with equipment. He had twin tanks on his back, a belt of hand tools round his waist, the phone on his chest, the new narrow beam searchlight held in one hand, its power cable lashed to the shot rope *Circe* would pay out. He waddled to the side and two of the crew helped him on to the ladder. The weather was still being kind. There was a slight swell but hardly any wind. Thomas went down the ladder till he was almost completely submerged. He stopped there and started a final check on his equipment.

Up on the bridge Bright and Ellam listened. The phone crackled and spoke through its amplifier. "Diver to *Circe*. Diver to *Circe*. Do you read me?"

"Loud and clear," said Johnny. "Now try that fancy light." He went out into the wing of the bridge and looked down into the water. The pencil beam sprang out under the surface and swung round in a wide arc.

Thomas's voice was enthusiastic. "Man, that's a grand light. Not much range in this water but anything's a help."

Ellam went back to the wheelhouse. "Right, Bert, check your compass and I'll give you a heading." They compared readings. Johnny put a searchlight on the marker buoy and took a bearing. With the tide turned, *Circe* was now north-east of the wreck, bow into the current. He corrected the bearing for the diver's compass. "Head 245, Bert. You got that? 245."

"245. O.K."

"And mind what I told you. That compass'll probably go wild when it gets close to all that steel down there."

"I've got it, Johnny. I'm ready to go."

Ellam spoke into the loud-hailer. "Stand by to slack that shot rope. You can go now, Bert."

"Good luck," said Bright and pressed the switch on the tape recorder.

Johnny looked at him. That's in character. You're the kind who always remembers to say the right things. Good luck, Bert Thomas, and please don't get caught down there before you find that nut Colney. What's so special about Colney? D'you think he's struck oil or something? Or is he just a good friend, like Brad is to me? But you're thorough, Bright. I'll give you that. God knows where you raked this gear up from at short notice. Even a tape recorder to make sure nothing's missed. I hate your guts already, Mr. Bright, but I'll admit you're thorough.

The tape hissed as the reels spun. The phone reported progress. The shaft of light was showing under the surface. The searchlights kept track of the rising bubbles. "Twenty feet—on course. Nothing showing yet." Roger was crouched at the amplifier. Ellam could hear the diver from his position at the wheelhouse window. He tried to trace Thomas's progress underwater as he jogged *Circe* with engines and rudder to hold her position close behind him.

"You were right, Johnny. Must be near now. This compass has gone mad. . . . No, nothing yet. . . . Wait, there's something, just below me. . . . Twenty-five . . . thirty feet now . . . Christ . . ."

"What is it, man?" barked Roger.

Nothing.

Ellam was across at the phone. "Bert, are you all right?"

"Yes, I'm all right, Johnny. Got a bit of a fright. It's a body. Yes, I see now. It's trapped. It looks like one of the rig's legs."

"That's the toolpusher. We know about him."

"You don't know nothing. Bodies don't scare me. It was that shoal of wee fishes. They were feeding on his face."

The only sound in the wheelhouse was the hiss of the tape.

"Do you want to come out?" asked Bright.

"Don't be bloody stupid."

Bright said nothing. Johnny watched the searchlight beams on the water, trying to forget these little fish.

"That's the top of the wreck then. Say twenty-five feet. Going down now . . . Forty . . . Fifty . . . Seventy . . . Eighty . . . Eighty-five and I can see bottom. . . . Johnny, that rope's dragging something awful. Come up on this side. If it's up and down it won't drag."

"Coming now. Keep in touch." Ellam spoke into the loud-hailer. "I'm going ahead. Haul in that rope and cable as it comes slack. And for God's sake keep it clear of the screws." He set the engines and the workboat moved ahead. The marker buoy was clear to starboard. He cut the engines. "I'm stopped again, Bert. How's that?"

"Better. Could do with a bit more."

"She'll drift up. Wait for it."

Half a minute. "Fine. Plumb up and down as far as I can see. That's not far down here, I can tell you, light or no light. I'm going up over the top to have a look. Haul in any slack you get. I don't want to get snagged."

Ellam put a fresh leaf of gum into his mouth and chewed on it. Roger was silent, waiting.

"Over it now. It's a hell of a mess. The derrick's right across the platform. Going down a bit now . . . wreckage everywhere . . . that must be it . . . yes, I see the hut . . . not a chance."

"What's that?" snapped Bright.

"I said not a chance, not from here anyway. The hut's smothered in wreckage. I'll go back round the side and try and find a way in."

The tape reels rotated. The small sound was loud to the waiting men.

"It's better here. I think I can get through to it now . . . maybe. . . . Back up, Johnny, that cable's on the wreck."

Ellam slammed the engine levers for a quick turn. *Circe* spun her stern to the south, away from the wreck. "Keep that rope tight."

"O.K., Johnny. I'm going in now. Just enough slack, not too much."

"I'll watch it, Bert."

A minute. "Now we'll see. I'm up to the bulkhead, about half-way along the hut. Hold it like that . . . hammer out . . . here we go."

In the wheelhouse they listened. When it came the noise was unexpectedly loud. Thud—thud—thud. There was a metallic tone to it.

"You've got something," shouted Roger. "There's someone there."

"There's someone here all right. It's me. That's my hammer you're hearing. The phone picks it up. Keep quiet now."

Thud—thud—thud. Nothing. Thud—thud—thud. Still nothing.

"Sounds empty. Doesn't sound like it's full of water. I'll try again." Thud—thud—thud . . . "Looks like we're out of luck."

"Keep trying, man," ordered Bright. "Colney's down there, I tell you. He's got to be."

"All right, all right. I'm still trying. I never said no one was down here. That toolpusher was down here. He wasn't talking."

Chapter 7

It was like his childhood all over again. The headaches had plagued Ted Colney then. They were worse at night, when the ache became real pain and his head felt like a bell with the clapper crashing to and fro inside. His father said it was growing pains, then that he studied too hard, did not get out in the fresh air, never played rough and tumble games like other boys. It was two years before his mother plucked up courage and took him to the doctor. He needed glasses. His father was furious. Only one son, a bit of a sissy, and now with steel-rimmed spectacles to mark him as less than a proper male. But the headaches disappeared.

Now they were back, thudding inside his head as he shook himself awake. He opened his eyes but saw nothing. Everything was black. Not black like darkness which is never total. This blackness was absolute. He blinked his eyes. Good lord, I'm blind. I can't see. Where am I? He felt around. He felt familiar shapes and textures but he could not see them. Then he started remembering. The rig. An explosion. Water all round. Tucker. Where was Tucker? "Tucker. Tucker." His shout echoed eerily. The thudding came again, hollow, metallic. There were other sounds. Snuffling, snoring, groaning. That must be Tucker. A light, I must have a light. He felt around and found a torch.

The beam split the blackness and relief swept over him. He remembered it all now. Nothing was frightening if there was no darkness. He saw Tucker on the bunk. His head was rolling from side to side. He was groaning and snorting in his sleep. His big face looked pale under the torch. Colney switched on the emergency lighting and the darkness was pushed farther back. The noise returned; thud—thud—thud. Colney looked around and shook his head. That wasn't inside me. That was somewhere else. He listened. There was nothing for half a minute then he heard it again. Three blows, regular, deliberate, muffled but distinct. Please, not another one trapped underneath here. Please, not another one to listen to and hear dying. But that's not the same kind of sound. That sound's different, nearer, controlled, demanding, not desperate. It's from outside. Tucker said they'd come looking for us. He shouted. "Here. In here." His voice leapt back at him from the bulkheads and the roof. That's no good. They'll never hear that. Must signal back. He scrambled across the debris towards the bulkhead. Where are they? No sounds now. I'm too late. They've gone away. They think there's no one here. He stumbled and fell, crawled on on all fours. He stretched out and struck at the bulkhead with the torch he still held. The panelling gave only a muted sound.

"What the hell're you doing?" Tucker was awake.

"There's someone outside." Colney beat on the panelling. "I told you, didn't I."

"Quiet." He listened. There was no reply. "I think they've gone away. They don't know we're here."

"Keep trying." Tucker hammered with his fist on the bulkhead where he lay.

Colney saw the metal bracket above his head connecting the side frame to the overhead beam. He struck at it and the steel sounded harsh and heartening. He pounded on it again and again.

"D'you hear anything?" bawled the Texan.

The shout stopped Colney's frantic hammering. "Shut up," he roared back. He put his ear to the bulkhead. After what seemed an age, he heard it. Thud—thud—thud.

77

He stayed huddled against the wall panels, gasping for breath, tears starting in his eyes.

"I heard something," shouted Tucker.

Colney nodded and sobbed.

"Get on with it, Limey. What's the matter with you? Hammer back."

The geologist wiped at his eyes and started hammering with the torch. From outside came the reply; not now the searching tap—tap—tap but a new pattern of blows, like Morse. Colney could not make sense of it.

"Don't just squat there. Do something."

"Shut up, will you." Colney listened. It came again, more slowly. He spelled it out. S-H-O-U-T. Could that be right? Of course, water is a superb conductor. If I shout, the diver will hear me. Seems silly till you think about it. "Hallo." The sound was earsplitting in the sealed chamber. One tap. Does that mean they heard me? We'll need a code. He yelled again. "One—tap—yes—two—taps—no." One tap. "Can—you—hear—me?" One tap, yes. He was panting. He breathed deeply to replace the air in his lungs. "Two—here—Colney—Tucker." The diver acknowledged. "Can—you—get—us—out?" The answer came back—yes. "How—long?" There was a pause, then five taps. "Five." One tap for yes. "Five—o'clock." No. "Five—hours." Yes. "Hurry—Tucker—broken—leg." One tap then a flurry of blows like a drum roll to end a dance tune. The diver was leaving.

Colney's throat was sore with shouting. He stayed crouched against the bulkhead, gasping for breath.

"Another five hours," growled Brad. "Was that right? They're sure taking their time."

"I suppose there's a lot to do. They'll need special equipment. I told them to hurry."

"Let's hope they do. This leg of mine's starting to hurt. What's the time now?"

Colney peered at his watch. "Just gone half past five." He thought about that. What half past five? Morning or evening? Must be morning unless I slept the clock round. Couldn't have done that. So it's half past five in the morning. Lord, only eight or nine hours since it all started yet it seems like a lifetime. So much for being so sure I could resign myself to dying down here alone. Maybe I could have, alone. People get in the way though. First Tucker, then that man down below in the pump-room, now that other man outside. Now it's not just simple acceptance of the inevitable, a welcome sight of the end of the road. No, now I may be rescued so I want to be rescued. I want to see daylight and moonlight, buildings, cars, boats, flowers, papers, food, everything. Yes, even people. Even Carol and the children whom I haven't seen for so long. Maybe them more than anything else.

"How long you going to stay perched over there like a monkey in the zoo?"

"Sorry, Tucker." He crawled back. "You were saying your leg hurt. I'll have a look at it."

"What was keeping you so quiet?"

"Nothing. I was thinking."

"What about?"

"This and that." Colney laughed. "Silly really. I had to think about whether it was morning or evening. There's no way of knowing down here."

Brad grunted. "What about this busted leg?"

Colney unwound the dressing. The bleeding had stopped and the flesh round the protruding bone was black with dried blood. The dressing was stained so he put on a fresh one. "That's about all I can do. How does it feel?"

"That one's not so bad. Can't you unstrap the other one?"

"Yes, I could do that. I'll have to splint this one, but it would let you move the right one about."

"Try that."

The geologist searched around for something to use as splints. He wrenched a couple of pieces off one of the lab benches and bound them into place. He massaged the

Texan's uninjured leg and then told him to try bending it.

Tucker grimaced with the pain of the blood surging back. The first movements were spasmodic but the muscles soon took full control. "That's better. With one leg in action I don't feel so bad."

"Just don't try too much. That other leg's not in very good shape."

"O.K., doc. Say, Colney, where'd you learn all this doctoring. You're pretty good."

"It's only first aid."

"You're turning out more useful than I'd have guessed. Your last night's plumbing seems to be holding out too."

"Good lord, I'd better check on that. I forgot." Colney got up and started moving round the hut.

"Must be all right," called Tucker. "We're still dry."

"I'll just check anyway." He inspected the inlet and outlet of the air conditioning. No sign of water now. He moved over to the sink against the outside bulkhead then into the bathroom.

He had known real fear the night before when Tucker had heard water seeping into the laboratory. Colney had started searching but at first could find nothing. Nothing but that untraceable sound which he had not noticed before but now imagined as a torrent. Then he found the tiny stream running out from behind the panelling. All the time he was calling back to Tucker. It was the Texan who thought of the air conditioning. No, it couldn't be that. The sirens had sounded and when the sirens sounded the air conditioning cut out and fireproof shutters closed over all the apertures. Fireproof yes, but were they waterproof? Were they waterproof ninety feet down under the sea where the pressure was almost four atmospheres? He had torn away the perforated screen with his bare hands. Tucker was right. There was water running in from the intake grille. Not a lot but enough to be an earnest of the vast sea outside. This was Tucker's kind of problem. He told Colney what to do. With what he could find amid the debris he made up a solid pad. He faced it with layer upon layer of rubber cut from a lab apron. Then, following the Texan's orders exactly, he shored the seal in place over the inlet and wedged the shoring tight. Next the outlet. With that sealed, the sound of water ceased. But there were other apertures they now remembered. Taps, sink outlets, shower drains, the soil pipe from the W.C. Colney had gone round them all, turning valves where there were valves, jamming plugs, sealing openings with anything he could find. None of them had shown any signs of seepage. There was no way of knowing if the pipes had been broken outside or how long the non-return valves on the drains would resist the massive pressure of the depth.

Now he discovered that everything was still in place. He went back to where Tucker was lying. "You were right. There's no sign of water."

"What'd I tell you? You're a good plumber, Colney. Hell, I'm hungry. What's for eating?"

"There's that steak that was for my supper last night. Would you like a bit of that?"

"Why not. We might as well fill up while we're waiting for that help to arrive."

The meat was cold and greasy and soiled but they both chewed it down and enjoyed it. A mouthful of the flat tasting distilled water completed their breakfast. Time—six-thirty. Four hours to wait.

"What will they do when they come back?" asked Colney. "How will they get us out of here?"

"Don't know. Just leave it to the experts. They'll get us out." Tucker was sucking on an unlit cigar. "One thing about all this, Colney. It's going to cure me of smoking."

"That's funny. I've just noticed."

"Just noticed what? It was you who told me about sucking them."

"No, not that. Something else."

"What now?"

Colney shivered and wrapped a blanket round himself. "Are you warm enough?"

"For crissake, Limey, what the hell've you just noticed?"

"There it is again. It's interesting how it changes with your mood. You called me Limey just now. That's what you've called me almost ever since we met. But a minute ago you were calling me Colney."

Brad heaved himself up off the mattress, winced with the pain and collapsed back again. "Jesus, you're a queer one. All that big build up and all it's about is what I call you. What the hell's it matter?"

"I don't suppose it does matter. But it is interesting. Why should you have changed?"

Tucker shook his head. "Maybe because Limey's an insult and I'm too smart to be nasty to someone I need as much as I need you now."

"That's honest at least."

Brad growled with disgust. "Now I guess I've hurt your Limey feelings again. What's it matter? I call you Colney, so what. That's the trouble with you eggheads. You always have to have reasons for things. You think too much." He closed his eyes to end the conversation.

"Maybe you're right." Ted Colney gave a small smile. He could see the big man was in more pain than he wanted to admit. He reminded him of his own father. That had been one of his pet remarks. "You think too much."

Big John, everyone had called him. Big John Colney. He had been a shot-firer in the quarry back home on the west side of the Pennines. He was a big man, with big muscles, a big appetite, a big thirst, and a big heart for everyone but his wife and son. No, that was not true. It was just that he only understood people and things on his scale at his level. His wife and son did not really fit this formula. Dora Colney was small and neat, like so many women attracted to big men. She had much the same background as Big John; they were both from the village. But Dora had worked up at the big house and had acquired a certain gentility. It was of no help with her husband. He delighted in being coarse and bawdy, in drink he forgot his own strength. He was not a cruel man. He was just strong. A playful punch from him could mark her with a bruise that lasted till next pay-day. He had primitive ideas about manliness. Sexual prowess was only part of it; the final proof was in the number of children fathered. With Dora, there was only one, young Ted. And he grew up into a disappointing half-boy.

John Colney had wanted more children as proof of his masculinity. None came. When his cronies told him his wife must be doing something to stop babies coming, he beat her. That did not work. In the end he found others to gratify him. There were no children that way but he enjoyed himself. And Dora was always there if he needed her. It never occurred to her to leave him. She was not the only wife in the village to be treated that way. She accepted it as part of the scheme of things. She had a roof over her head, she had her son, her man was in work so there was always enough to eat and fuel for the fire. In the twenties that was a lot to be thankful for.

Young Ted was bright at school. He had these headaches but even so he was always top of the class. After he got his glasses and the headaches went away, there was no keeping him in books. He played with other children but he was small and shortsighted and easily reduced to tears. He was always glad to escape to his books. He asked questions all the time. He took nothing for granted. Only a reasoned explanation would satisfy him. His mother had not the knowledge or wit to keep pace with him; his father had not the patience. "You think too much." But it was his father who gave Ted Colney his interest in rocks. Big John would take his son up to the quarry to see the shot firing. The man was proud of that huge cliff, of the noise and dust of the drills, the suspense of the shot placing, the roar and rumble of the explosives and the sundered mountain. The boy was frightened by it all. But when the dust settled and the noise had echoed away to nothing, he saw the tumble of stone and gazed in awe at the colour and complexity of the rock, compressed, torn, pushed up, heated, frozen, eroded by wind and water for millions of years. He looked at it, he fingered it. "It's stone, son. Fine stone, building stone, that's all you need to know." But young Ted needed to know much more. He was still at the village school but now he knew what he was going to be.

He had never from that day thought about any other career than geology. From the village school he went on to the county secondary school. He mixed with other children as little as he could. Boys were always fighting; girls embarrassed him. He played no games but he learned how to defend himself. He had inherited his strong arms from his father and he soon found out that his crushing grip could save him from violence. He won a scholarship to the grammar school and put off for days telling his father about it, trying to catch him in a good humour for he knew that Big John would not be impressed with further proof of his son's brains. But he was wrong. Big John had to be proud. If he could not be proud of his son as a man as he understood men, he was happy to be proud of him as a brainy one. He boasted of it at the pub, laughed when his friends said that his brains had all slipped down into his trousers, brought beer home to initiate his son, and made him drink it till Ted was sick all over the hearth.

Grammar school meant staying away in lodgings. It was all paid for so Big John was better off than before with one less mouth to feed. His son was turning out very well. It was as if he was earning already. Dora was not so sure. She was proud that her boy was going to be better than her husband but she missed him at home. And she saw him changing. With each holiday time she saw the significant changes, the way he ate, the way he spoke, the way he looked at the shabby furniture, the way he looked at her. She never fathomed that, the way he looked at her. She thought he was becoming ashamed of her and his home. It was not that. He felt no shame. He had just lost interest. His new environment was different and he felt more at home in it. What he felt for his mother when he went home was pity; pity for the way she accepted her lot, pity for the smallness of her world. But Ted Colney as a youth was no better at expressing his emotions than later as an adult. So he stayed aloof and plunged himself into his work. He did well. He won a free place at the university. 1938.

The war came at the end of his first year but he was allowed to finish his degree. His eyes saved him from the fighting but he made maps for the Army. It kept his hand in at surveying and allowed him time to develop his ideas about the earth's crust. He kept himself to himself, drank little, womanised not at all. He had a good war but it was a different good war from other soldiers'. Demobilised he went back to the university with a grant to do a Ph.D. That behind him he won a research grant and his papers began to be noticed in the world of geology. He was a Doctor of Science by the time he was thirty-two. That year he met Carol.

Carol was different. She was twenty, not beautiful but striking, intense about everything she did, and given to hero-worship. She was starting her final year. She came to his tutorials and worked in the laboratory. She had brains and he encouraged her. She admired Ted's work and it was soon obvious that she admired him too. He was aghast at feeling himself being drawn into the vortex of a personal relationship but it was a new kind of experience for him. Carol was a new kind of woman; with her it would be different. And so it was. For a year or two.

They were married as soon as she graduated. He never took her to see his parents. He had not been home since the end of the war. He felt no shame or bitterness about them; he just had nothing in common with them. He found it easier to close doors behind him. He went on with his research and they set up house near the university. It was a marvellous time. What better can there be than two people whose minds blend and stimulate at one and the same time? Bodies too for this was not just a marriage of minds.

Ted Colney smiled to himself as he remembered. Then the smile faded. The good time had not lasted long.

"What's so funny?" Tucker's question startled him.

"Nothing, nothing. Why do you ask?"

"Just wondered. You were grinning like to bust. I thought maybe I'd like the joke too."

"No. I was just thinking about my wife."

"Your wife?" The Texan started to laugh but his mirth was cut short by a spasm of coughing.

Colney moved over and propped him up and patted his back. "Easy, easy."

Tucker drew breath and lay panting in the scientist's arms. "You threw me, Limey. I—I never thought—thought you was the—the marrying type."

"Take it easy. Don't speak. Just get your breath back."

Brad lay still for a minute and his breathing eased. "Thanks. That's better."

Ted eased him back down on to the bunk and went back to his place. He was angry at himself for letting slip the mention of his wife. He had never talked of her to anyone for a long time. Tucker was the last man he would have wanted to know.

"Say, Colney. Have you noticed anything?"

"No, what?"

"That coughing fit, for one. And we're both breathing sort of fast. Now I can't smell the tobacco in this end I'm chewing."

Colney stared at him, watched his breathing, listened to his own, sniffed. "You're right, of course. That's why we can't smell. It's the CO_2. Carbon dioxide."

"Give me credit. I know what CO_2 is. Where's it coming from? It's poisonous, ain't it."

"It's coming from us. We're breathing it out all the time. We're sealed in here. We're breathing it back in."

Tucker grimaced. "That's nice. Anything to do?"

"No. Just wait till they come for us. Don't talk, don't move about. Try and sleep. You breathe less then."

"I don't know about sleep, Limey, but I'll not be moving about with this busted leg." He smiled wanly. "What's the time?"

"Half seven."

"Three hours till they come for us. Can we last out?"

Colney shook his head. "I don't know. Maybe."

Chapter 8

H.M.S. *Blackamoor* was at full speed. The frigate had logged a steady twenty-two knots since clearing the bridges outside Rosyth. The weather had been kind; calm in the Forth with a few small patches of mist but clear since the Bass Rock, the breeze from the north-east sweeping away any chance of fog but only stirring the sea into occasional white caps on top of the low swell. It was seven-thirty in the morning, Sunday. *Blackamoor* was still ninety miles short of Offshore Five's position.

Commander Gaile was awake before the steward called him and put the china mug of steaming coffee into his hands. He was awake and lying in the two arm-chairs in the wardroom which he had made into a makeshift bed. He was enjoying the feel of being on a ship at sea again. This was a bonus for him. He had looked forward to his trip to the Clyde depot for he knew he would meet submariners he knew and had not seen for some time down at the shore command at Gosport. But apart from that he had expected to be talking, lecturing and inspecting all the time. The one trip he had taken was only up the loch to fire a few torpedoes down the range. Tame stuff.

He threw off the blankets and pushed away the chair holding his legs. He sipped his coffee and got up and stretched. He was still in uniform. He grinned. Feel better sleeping in my clothes. More like the old days. Frank Gaile had been in submarines for almost all his twenty-five years' service. He would have preferred to be in them still but at least he was still concerned with them.

He was not one to admit that he was too old but he was grateful that the submarine service still needed experienced men to instruct and to test. His speciality was escape systems. The night before, when the call came for the portable recompression chamber and a diving team to rush through to Rosyth for this oil rig wreck in the North Sea, he had jumped at the chance. Lieutenant Strang and his divers were delighted to have him with them.

The settee where Strang and the team doctor had been sleeping was empty. They're keen ones, thought Gaile. They'll be up there on deck making sure the chamber's still there and checking all the other gear. Admirable but unnecessary. That call last night was proof enough they know what they're about. Couldn't have done better myself. That call from Rosyth was at 2215. Fifteen minutes later the chamber, sitting ready on its trailer for just such an emergency, was on its way. Ten minutes after that the team was in two trucks with all its gear and chasing the trailer. Two divers were missing; they had the evening off. These two were wending their way unsteadily back to base. The sight of the trailer sobered them up and they were there at the roadside waiting for the trucks to pick them up. The base had wasted no time either. A police patrol met the convoy west of Glasgow and from there on it had been non-stop, lights flashing, sirens wailing to clear the road. They had taken the main Edinburgh road for most of the way, then cut off to cross the Forth Road Bridge to Rosyth. *Blackamoor* was there with a crane along-side ready to lift the chamber on board. In a quarter of an hour the frigate was letting go her lines. Little more than two hours from that first call. Pretty swift by any standards.

The steward came back to ask Gaile if he would take breakfast with the captain. Gaile said yes and went up to eat bacon and eggs in the tiny cabin. *Blackamoor*'s captain was a lieutenant-commander in his early thirties. Gaile outranked him but still showed him the respect he felt due to anyone in command. He called him Captain and the

Captain called him Sir. They soon agreed on how to handle the rescue. Gaile would control the diving and rescue work and the young captain would work the frigate, taking the older man's advice on what was necessary to help with the work underwater. That suited Frank Gaile. He had never bothered very much about promotion. He could be very down-to-earth. He had made Commander but he knew he would go no further. Most of the time he felt no bitterness. It was the luck of the draw. He had a job, a job he liked doing. That was more than a lot of people could say. He wondered about the young captain. Would he jump the barrier to Commander then on to the rarefied level of Captain and beyond? Good luck to him. He'll need it. He looks like the kind who gets another ulcer with each stripe.

After breakfast the commander went up on the bridge to get a breath of air. The frigate was slicing open the grey sea and the wind from the beam was whipping spume up from the curling bow wave and across the decks. The cloud was high, with about a nine-tenths coverage, but thin enough to show where the sun was with a big bright patch. Gaile filled his lungs with the salt-tinged air. It not only felt good. If this weather held, the rescue could be just like a simple exercise. But he knew that the weather was a small factor. The real problems turned on how these men were entombed, where they were entombed, what access was available, how fit they were to co-operate. There was a problem even more basic; would these men still be alive when the divers got to them? Even if they were, this was a new kind of problem. Getting men out of a wrecked submarine was one thing. At least a submarine was built with the idea of making escape possible. And submariners had some idea of what was required. Most of them had been up through the Gosport tank. Who were these men down in the wreck of that oil rig? Were they injured? Again, that basic question; would they still be alive?

Gaile went down to Plot to have a look at the chart.

A quarter to nine. Still more than sixty miles to go. Say three hours. About noon. He picked up Strang and asked permission to use the R/T. They went along together and told the operator to call *Circe*.

Ellam's voice came back through the loudspeaker. "*Circe* calling *Blackamoor*. Receiving you loud and clear. Go ahead."

The commander took the microphone. "*Blackamoor* calling *Circe*. Commander Gaile here. Who am I speaking to?"

"Ellam."

"Are you the captain?"

"That's right."

"Good morning, Captain Ellam. We're about three hours from your position now. I just want to ask a few questions. It may help us to save a little time when we get there."

"Fire ahead."

"How many men are trapped down there?"

"Just two as far as we know. Our diver used up his time finding them but that's all we expected."

"How deep are they?"

"Between eighty and ninety feet."

"What kind of compartment are they in?"

"They're in the geology hut. It's a sort of deckhouse."

"It must be quite a deckhouse if it's keeping out the water at that depth."

"That's right. It's a bit special."

"Can you give me its size?"

"Hold on. I'll get it." Gaile doodled on his pad while he waited. Ellam came back on. "It's about sixteen by twelve by eight. Feet, that is."

"Yes, I've got that, Captain." He scribbled down the answer. About fifteen hundred cubic feet. "When were you last in touch?"

"Half five. We told them five hours then. You're going to be late."

"Sorry about that. We're shaking out rivets getting to you. How were they then?"

"Are you kidding, Commander? They certainly weren't telling funny stories. But they were alive. One of them's got a broken leg though."

"I see. Captain, could we use your ship to dive from. There's a lot of gear. Have you got deck space?"

"There's plenty of space. And you're welcome."

"Thanks very much. I'll see you about twelve noon. You've helped a lot."

"Anything to oblige the Navy. By the way, you won't get to that hut all that easily. The drilling derrick's collapsed right across it."

"That's not so good. But thanks for telling me. I'll plan for that. Good-bye, Captain."

"Bye and out."

The two officers walked back to the wardroom and sat down at the table. "What do you think, Lieutenant?" asked Gaile.

"It doesn't sound too bad, sir."

The commander shook his head. "No, not till you start thinking about it. This one might prove pretty tough. Take that hut. Two men, one and a half thousand cubic feet. Sounds a lot of air. But they'll have been in there more than fifteen hours when we get to them. We could work it out but I'd guess there won't be much useful air left by then. They'll be pretty far through."

Strang nodded slowly. "I suppose that's right."

"And just remember, Lieutenant. We can do nothing for them if they can't help us from inside."

Circe was drifting north of the marker buoy. Ellam was hunched up in his swing chair on the bridge He chewed slowly on a wad of gum and occasionally ran his eyes round from beam to beam. The sea was deserted. He had had a couple of hours sleep after the diver surfaced but he had come back to the bridge after breakfast to give the bosun a spell below. Johnny was not tired; he did with less sleep than most people but in any case he had had a few hours before Bright arrived. He was not tired but he felt jaded. Give him something to do and he got on with it. Order him to wait when he knew he could be doing something, then his quick temper would boil inside him and keep him sharp. But this kind of waiting, just floating about on the surface, not being able to do a thing to help that pair far below, this knocked the spirit right out of him.

He grimaced and rolled the gum into the other side of his mouth. Wish I was like Bright. No, that's not true. Wouldn't wish that on my worst enemy. But I've got to admit that he's got something. He's like a bloody machine. As soon as Bert Thomas was out of the water and had filled in the details on what went on down there, his lordship says he's going to get his head down. "Call me when you hear from the Navy, Johnny," he says. Then when I take him below and show him my bunk, he kicks off his shoes, rolls in and, hey presto, he's asleep. Uncanny, that was. Just as if he'd pressed a button. Not as if he looked dead beat. Quite the opposite. Like a dog with two tails, knowing that he'd been right from the beginning, that Colney and Brad were down there and alive. But excited or not, he still switched on sleep like I switch on the radar. He's quite something all right but I still don't like him. He's too free with the smooth talk and the first names. Everyone's a puppet to him, to control with a flick of the fingers, to put words into their mouths. I've got news for you, Roger. Johnny Ellam doesn't dance to anyone's tune. "Call me when you hear from the Navy, Johnny," he says. Well, I've heard from the Navy and I've not called you and I'm not going to. Sleep on and dream about how marvellous you are. I don't suppose you know you snore. That's one mistake you made, popping off to sleep like that when I was still in the cabin. Yes, Roger boy, you snore something awful. And that's something even the great Bright can't manage. To keep people in awe of you when they've seen you sleeping and snoring like a great sow.

Ellam put the gum out of his mouth and flicked it expertly through the wheelhouse door and over the side. The boat's bow had fallen off the wind and she was rolling gently in the small sea. He gave her a touch ahead with the engines and brought her back into the wind. Almost eleven o'clock. Another hour till the Navy arrives. Brad and Colney will be wondering what's happening. Poor old Brad. A broken leg. He'll be hopping mad or whatever it is you are when you can't hop. That'll teach the old bastard a lesson. No girls for a few weeks. Some hopes; he'll be in hospital surrounded by girls. I can't see Brad Tucker being put off by a chunk of plaster.

Well, he'll deserve all he can get after that lot down there. Must be hellish. They'll be in the dark, I suppose. Cold too and their air must be getting pretty stale by now. How long? Almost fourteen hours. And with that nut of a geologist too. God, but Brad hates that man's guts. That must be a cheery little party down there at the bottom of the sea. If only I could let him know the Navy'll soon be here. Wait a minute. What about the engines? That's what happens in these submarine films. They can hear a ship's propeller overhead. That's worth a try. If he hears them he'll know something's happening up here. Even if he doesn't it'll keep me busy. Why didn't I think of that before? I've been sitting here mooning the morning away when I could have been doing something. He slipped out of the chair and pushed both the engine levers to Full Ahead.

He did not see the plane coming in from the west. He was intent on manœuvring *Circe* near the orange float that the diver had left on his shot line to mark the hut. He hung out of the wheelhouse window, watching the float on the grey water, revving both engines, first ahead, then astern, then ahead again. He felt better. It was almost as if he was talking to Brad. Then he heard the noise of the plane. He snapped the engines to Stop and ran out into the wing of the bridge. The plane was end on, twin-engined, and diving straight at him. Johnny crouched instinctively as it flattened out and swooped noisily overhead, not more than fifty feet above him. He turned and ran through to the other side. He was shouting to no one in particular. "What the hell's that silly bugger think he's doing?" He watched as the plane banked and came in again. This time it flew in level then rounded *Circe* in a banking turn. The R/T was talking. "Hallo down there. Any news for the Press? We got some good photos. We can just see the shadow of the rig from up here."

Ellam shouted into the set. "Get off the air, will you. We're waiting for the Navy. Go and get your pictures somewhere else." He wanted to say a lot more. His fists were balled as he struggled to control himself. What did they think this was? Some kind of circus, some kind of stunt that was good for a headline. Didn't they know there were two men down there on the bottom getting closer to death with every minute that passed?

"Take it easy, old chap. We're only doing our job. The Navy won't be long now. We can see them from up here."

"Thanks. Now get off this frequency." Johnny flicked the set off. The plane did one more circuit then flew away to the north. That's right, go and take some pictures of the Navy. I hope they shoot you down in flames.

"What's all the rumpus about?" It was Bright, wakened by the noise of the plane, and standing at the wheelhouse door rubbing the sleep from his eyes.

"It was a plane load of press men," Johnny told him. "Looking for gory details."

Roger looked round at the retreating plane. "Good, it's nice they haven't forgotten us. It always helps to keep Inoco in the news. Did you talk to them?"

"I did."

"What did you tell them?"

"I told them to get to hell out of here and leave us alone."

Bright made a face. "You shouldn't have done that, Johnny. It's their job, you know."

"That's what they said."

"This is news. They'll be back. And they'll want to see you when you get ashore. When you're news, Johnny, you have to learn to live with reporters. They're not a bad bunch. You'd like them. They can take a fair bucket."

"Thanks. I'll buy my own drinks."

Roger was staring at the clock. "Is that the time? Good heavens, it's late. Where's that Navy ship? It should've been here by now."

"It's on the way. That plane said he could see it. It's due about noon. Ship called *Blackamoor*. I talked to her earlier on."

"You talked to it? Didn't I tell you to call me when the Navy got in touch?"

Ellam put a cigarette in his mouth and lit it before answering. "I didn't know you told me anything, Mr. Bright. I thought you just asked." He blew a cloud of smoke across the wheelhouse. "They only wanted to ask a few questions. They were simple. I managed to answer them. I thought maybe you could do with the extra sleep."

"Sorry," said Bright with a smile. "That was very good of you, Johnny. Has anything else . . ."

"Say, Skipper." It was the helmsman. "We're right on top of that buoy."

"Damn and blast." Ellam pushed Bright aside and ran into the wing of the bridge. The marker buoy was bumping along *Circe*'s side. Easy now. Bert said the top of the rig was more than twenty feet down. We don't draw that much so we shouldn't foul the wreck. Let her drift that buoy clear. The buoy bumped gently along the side and clear of the bow. Christ, what about that orange float? Did I overrun it? No, there it is. Thank God for that. Ellam put the engines Dead Slow Ahead and ran the workboat out from on top of the rig. He took her round to the north

96

again where the tide would keep her off. He stopped the engines. "What were you saying?" he asked Bright.

"Yes, what was I saying?" Roger scratched his head. "Oh, yes. Did anything else happen when I was asleep? Any messages?"

"No. I called the base after the Navy called me. I thought they should know what was going on."

"That's good. They had nothing for me?"

"Only that one of the roughnecks died before they got him to hospital."

"That's a pity."

"And the papers are full of us, of course."

"That's inevitable. Oil shares will take a knock to-morrow when the Exchange opens. It's very sensitive about the North Sea nowadays."

"I'm sure it can afford it." Ellam hitched himself up into his chair. He wished Bright would go away. He was wondering how to get rid of him when the cook arrived with coffee and gave him the lead he needed. "Cooky, take Mr. Bright down and get him some breakfast. He's just got up."

"Coffee's fine for me," said Roger. "But I could do with a shave."

"Try my cabin. There's an electric razor if that's any use."

"That'll be fine." He turned to go. "Oh, Johnny, you will call me when the Navy arrives."

"I'll call you. Take your time." Ellam plucked the glasses out of their box and focused on a tiny blemish on the horizon to the north-west. It was *Blackamoor*, end on, still hull down, but coming fast.

Chapter 9

The diving team on *Blackamoor* had been busy. The six divers and Lieutenant Strang were all suited up and ready to go. The racks of air bottles for the surface demand diving equipment were ready for transfer to *Circe*. Cutting equipment, telephones, shot ropes, marker buoys, listening gear, bolt guns, armoured hoses, all the paraphernalia of underwater rescue was stacked on deck. The rubber Gemini boat was inflated, its outboard motor fuelled, tested, and ready for shipping. A signals team from the frigate was briefed and standing by with walkie-talkies.

Frank Gaile wanted to be ready for anything. This was the kind of thing that needed quick decisions and quick decisions meant that the gear had to be there to hand. He had thought about the problems that might come up but he had tried to keep his mind free of assumptions. He wanted his men to get down there and get the picture for him. Time itself meant nothing. Success was all that mattered. Time was only important initially. These men down there would need air and they would need it in a hurry. That was the one decision he had made. Locate this hut and get fresh air into it. After that he would decide how to get them out.

He stood on *Blackamoor*'s bridge, away from the watch and the captain, taking no part in the approach, studying *Circe* through the glasses. She's a handy looking ship. Just what I need for this job. She looks like an American design. Lovely long run of deck aft. Here she comes now.

He saw the bow wave growing round the workboat's bluff bow. I wonder what her captain's like. He sounded all right. Where the hell's this wreck? I can't see a thing. Surely one of these big rigs would still show something above the surface. Not this one. Wait, there's a dan buoy. That must be it. *Circe* had turned and was lying fine on the frigate's bow. That's what I like to see. That skipper knows what he's doing. He's showing us the way and letting us do the work. Gaile glanced round at the sea to check the wind. North-east about Force 3. That's right, we'll go east of the wreck and turn up into the wind. Port side to the wreck so I want *Circe* on that side. He walked forward and discussed it with the frigate's captain who nodded agreement.

Gaile was down on deck when *Blackamoor* ran up on the workboat. He bellowed "Port side" through the hand hailer, saw the wave of acknowledgment, and nodded with pleasure as *Circe* let the slowing frigate pass her then leapt ahead under the warship's stern to come up on the port side. Before *Blackamoor* started her turn, *Circe* was made fast alongside and the first load was already in the air. Commander Gaile was on to the workboat's deck and on his way up to the bridge by the time the load landed.

Ellam was waiting for him. "Hallo there. I'm Ellam."

"I'm Gaile. We spoke a while back." *Circe*'s captain was younger than he had expected. "You've got a trim little ship, Captain. I like the way you handle her."

"Thanks. She's all right. Come on in and tell me what you want done." Johnny led the way into the wheelhouse. Bright was there. "Commander Gaile, Mr. Bright. Mr. Bright's the boss man from London."

They shook hands. "Glad to know you, Mr. Bright," said Gaile. "How is it you're out here?"

"I came out by helicopter as soon as I heard about the rig."

"Rather you than me. I can't stand the things myself. But it's good you're here. It helps to have someone to liaise with. You'd be surprised the trouble we run into for doing this kind of thing without official permission."

"I can't believe it."

"It's true though. Now, gentlemen, let's get down to business. Have you drawings of the rig, especially this hut?"

"Here they are." Roger handed them over.

"Good. Now, Captain, is that dan buoy marking the wreck?"

"That's right. And our diver left his shot rope tied on down there. There's an orange float on it. Can you see?"

Gaile lifted his binoculars. "Got it. That was a bright idea." He swung the glasses round. "I'd hoped there would be some of the wreck showing. We'll have to moor somehow."

"I could anchor but I'll have to head into the wind. As it is now an anchor would foul the wreck. How about the wreck though. As you say. Our diver said the top is only twenty feet down. We could run a line."

"Will it hold, d'you think?"

"Should do, Old Offshore Five went in hard. She won't shift easily."

"Good," said Gaile. "We'll run one of your mooring lines. Our divers'll place it. Bring the end back on board and we'll be ready to slip if we have to."

"What about the stern? There's a tide here, you know."

"Have you got a kedge?"

"I've got a spare bower. It'd do but I haven't got enough wire."

"That's soon fixed." Gaile went out into the wing and hailed the frigate's captain. "Captain, we need some wire for a kedge. Send it over in a cutter. And lash on a single batten for dropping the kedge." He turned back to Ellam. "How much wire? Depth's about fifteen, isn't it? Say, seventy, eighty fathoms?"

"That should do."

Gaile shouted back to the frigate. "Eighty fathoms.

Eight Oh." He came back into the wheelhouse. "Good, gentlemen, we're getting on like a house on fire. Now let's look at these plans." He opened up the sheet. It was huge so he took it through to the chartroom and spread it. Ellam and Bright joined him.

"That's the hut there," said Johnny. "You'll see it's up on a deck of its own down towards the point of the triangle. The rig fell with that point down."

"I see. Is there a separate plan of the hut itself?"

"Yes, down here." Ellam shifted the sheet and pointed.

The commander studied it carefully. "You were right, Captain. That's some deckhouse. These are watertight doors, eh. Must be damned good to stay tight at that depth."

"They're pretty hefty. They've got swing handles all the way round."

"I see there's a sort of sealed compartment between these doors." He stabbed his finger at Colney's vestibule.

"Looks like it," said Johnny. "I've never been inside."

"It is like that, Commander," put in Bright. "I remember it. It's like a little hallway."

"Thanks. That might be useful later on." Gaile pushed his cap up off his forehead. "Gentlemen, these two men have been down there fifteen hours now. There's not much good air left. They'll be pretty groggy if they're still alive. I plan to get air to them first, then take a good look round, then decide how to get them out. Is that agreed?"

"You're the expert."

"Yes, of course," said Roger. "But can't we just get them out right away?"

Gaile smiled wryly. "I haven't got a magic wand, Mr. Bright."

"No, but isn't there some sort of chamber you were bringing?"

"There is, it's on the frigate. But it's for after, when we get them out, if we get them out. Believe me, this may take quite a bit of time."

"I see." Roger wanted to ask how long was quite a bit of time. These options had less than thirty hours to run. He had to talk to Ted Colney before then.

The commander was watching him. "There's not a time limit, is there, Mr. Bright?"

"No, no, of course not. Just the sooner the better."

"Don't worry, Mr. Bright. I won't waste any time. But I won't take unnecessary risks either."

"Quite right. The important thing's to get him out alive."

"Him? I thought there were two of them."

"Yes, there are. Sorry, I just happened to be thinking of Colney. I—I know him rather well."

Gaile nodded. "I understand." He saw Ellam, his mouth set in a hard line. The air in the little chartroom felt charged.

Lieutenant Strang's arrival broke the tension. "Everything's loaded, sir. We're setting up now."

"Thanks, Strang. Come in. This is Lieutenant Strang, gentlemen. He's in charge of the diving team. Captain Ellam. Mr. Bright." They all nodded to each other. "We're ready if you are, Captain."

Johnny went out to the bridge. The frigate was round into the wind and stopped. He signalled to let go. *Blackamoor*'s men let the lines go and Ellam sheared the workboat away to port. He took *Circe* to the south in a tight turn then rounded again to come up on the buoy with his bow into the breeze which had stiffened and was chopping the water into a myriad of white crests.

Gaile had quickly told the lieutenant what he had found out and what he wanted done. "So that's it. As soon as we're in position, send the Gemini off to find the shallow bit of the wreck and run a line to it. Then two men down that shot rope to scout this hut."

"Right you are, sir. That diver who was down this morning was useful. He's genned the lads up on what to expect. There's quite a bit of wreckage apparently."

"That's not surprising."

"Will they take the Cox's down with them, sir?"

"No, leave that bolt gun up here. We can send it down when we're ready."

Strang went back to his men. The commander folded up the plans of the rig and went through to the wheelhouse. He leaned on the window ledge.

"How about the weather, Commander?" asked Bright.

"This is fine," said Gaile. "We can take it a good deal rougher than this." He spoke without turning round. He was trying to think himself into the problem of getting these men up out of the wrecked rig. He wanted no interruptions. The whole thing was going to hinge on the way the hut was lying. If it lay just right, it could be simple. If it didn't, it might prove very difficult.

He watched as Ellam conned *Circe* into position and the Gemini boat went away with the divers to lay the bow mooring. The signalman on the walkie-talkie reported the mooring laid round one of the submerged legs. Ellam backed the workboat down till the orange float was alongside. A sailor hooked it and hauled it on board. The commander spoke to Ellam. "I'm going down on deck, Captain. Maybe you'd like to join me when you've got that stern mooring out."

"I'll do that."

"Are you coming down, Mr. Bright?"

"Yes, I'll come now."

From the ladder Gaile saw the frigate's cutter paying wire on to the workboat's deck. The spare anchor was already hanging on a tackle from the stern davit. No worries up here about co-operation. Now let's find out if this pair down on the bottom are fit to co-operate.

Strang had everything ready. The telephones and listening gear were grouped into a control post in the lee of the superstructure. The first two divers were ready. Gaile briefed them. They went over into the water and the Gemini drifted down wind to stand by for emergencies. The commander moved over out of the wind and leaned against a bulkhead. He lit a cigarette in cupped hands and listened as Strang tested the telephones, checked the air supply, and reported the descent. The tape recorders were running.

"What are these hoses for?" asked Bright.

"Surface Demand, we call it. It's air for the divers."

"But they had tanks on their backs. Aren't they for breathing?"

"Yes, but that puts a limit on their time below. When we can we give them air from these bottles on deck. That way there's virtually no limit. Their back tanks are for emergencies."

"They're down, sir," reported the lieutenant. "They think they're right on target. That shot rope made it easy."

"Good. Is there room to work?"

Strang relayed the question. "Yes, sir. Enough. The hut's at eighty-five feet. Bottom's ninety-seven."

"Tapping on Sonar, sir," reported the man on the listening gear.

"What the hell are they doing, Strang?"

"It's all right, sir. They were just checking to see if the compartment's filled. It's not. That looks like the right one."

"We knew it was," said Gaile testily. "Tell them to do what they're told. Only what they're told. Send down that loudspeaker." He puffed on his cigarette then stamped it out. He waited.

"Speaker's in place, sir."

"Good. Now just in case this thing's as good as these boffins on the Clyde claim, tell them to plug their ears."

"Ready, sir."

The commander took the microphone and signed to the Sonar man to turn his volume down. "What are their names, Mr. Bright?"

"Colney and Tucker."

"Thanks." He took a deep breath. "Hallo there. Hallo there. Hallo, Mr. Colney. Hallo, Mr. Tucker. This is the Navy here. If you are hearing this, tap three repeat three times." The whole control party was tense. The Sonar man had the volume full up, his eyes narrowed in concentration. Then he shook his head. Gaile started again. "Hallo there. Hallo there. . . ." After the third attempt he checked his watch. It was after one o'clock. Almost sixteen hours. They'll be pretty weak even if they're still concious. Keep trying. "Hallo there. Hallo there. . . ." The Sonar man had a finger up. Two, three, four—he ran out of fingers. Gaile spoke again. "Hallo there. We hear tapping. If you are reading this, tap five repeat five times."

All eyes were on the man on the listening gear. One, two, three, four, five. Somebody cheered and there was excited chatter. "Shut up," roared the commander. He glared round the group. "Send down the Cox's, Mr. Strang. And tell them to wait till they're told to use it."

"Yes, sir."

"Hallo there. Hallo there. We are going to give you fresh air. Listen carefully. Please lie down flat. We will fire two bolts through the shell of the hut. These bolts have armour-piercing heads. When you are told, you must unscrew these heads. I repeat. Unscrew the heads but only when I tell you. One bolt will then deliver air, the other bolt will exhaust stale air up here to the surface. I will repeat these instructions. If you understand them, please tap four repeat four times." He went through it all again, speaking slowly and precisely into the microphone.

The Sonar man's fingers rose. One, two, three, four.

Gaile nodded and smiled. "Put in the bolts, Lieutenant."

"Eh, Commander, what about the thickness of the plate?"

Gaile swore. "I must be mad. Forgot all about that. Where are these plans? Tell them to wait, Strang." He unfolded the plans and spread them against the bulkhead.

"Damn and blast. It's all smeared. Might be half-inch, might be quarter. What about the joints? A lap joint would give a double thickness. No, they're all welded butts. Not even a doubler on the other side."

"What about these frames, sir? They'll give us a double thickness if we can find them."

"Good man, Strang. That's it. That one there. Near the end. Tell the divers to tap for it. It's about three feet from the end of the hut."

"Right, sir."

Gaile waited then signalled that he was going to use the loudspeaker again. "Hallo there. Hallo there. You will hear tapping. Do not worry. It will be the divers checking for a position to fire the bolts."

"They're on that now, sir," said the lieutenant.

"Good. Thank God you remembered, Strang. I must be getting dull in the head."

"I don't know what reminded me, sir. But suddenly I remembered reading about that one they fired a bolt into and it went straight through the other side."

"I know. They were lucky. There was no one inside still alive."

Strang held up a hand. "They've got it, sir."

"Right. Give me the mike. Hallo there. Hallo there. We are firing now. Do not, repeat not, touch these bolts till I tell you." He nodded to the lieutenant who spoke into the telephone.

They watched the Sonar operator. One finger raised. The first bolt had fired. Strang nodded. The divers reported the first bolt in place. Everyone waited. The divers would be reloading the gun and running up the lock nut on the first bolt. Second bolt fired. Divers report second bolt in place.

"Hoses down, Mr. Strang." The commander walked over to Roger. "Well, Mr. Bright, part one is almost over."

"Congratulations, Commander. You chaps certainly know what you're doing. I'm very impressed."

Gaile smiled. "Wait till you see the bill."

In five minutes Strang reported both hoses connected.

The commander took the microphone again. "Hallo there. Hallo there. Can you find the two bolts? Tap three times for yes."

Three taps reported.

"Good. Now unscrew the heads of the bolts. Tap five times when both, repeat both, heads are off."

There was a long delay. These bolt heads'll be tight for men short of air. Not men. One man. The other's got a broken leg. At last, five taps.

"Give them air, Mr. Strang," Gaile beckoned to Roger Bright. They went over to the side and the commander crouched down beside a small pump and lit a cigarette. He drew on it till it glowed brightly. "Watch this." He held the cigarette to the pump outlet. The glowing end dimmed then went black. Gaile put it back in his mouth and drew hard on it to prove it was out. "It's good for dousing fires, is CO_2. That's what your men have been breathing, Mr. Bright."

Roger whistled. "Will they be all right?"

"Should be. In half an hour or so that air down there will be as fresh as daisies. Half an hour after that they'll be as right as rain. It's tougher than most people think, the human body."

"I suppose that's true."

Ellam was there, grinning from ear to ear. "I hear you're through to them, Commander. That didn't take long. Sorry I missed it."

"We were just in time, Captain. Now they're getting air, we can take time to find the best way to get them out." Gaile smiled. "You've been busy yourself. I see you've got her all moored up."

"Yes, she seems all right for the time being. It wasn't much trouble with your boys to help us."

The commander walked over to the starboard side. The wind was coming from the bow but not too broad out.

Circe was riding the small sea easily. *Blackamoor* was moored too now, less than a cable's length to the east. Gaile stood for a moment enjoying the wind on his face. A boat was on its way across from the frigate. "That looks like the Doc. He's been testing the recompression chamber. Now he'll want to know how these two down there are making out."

"What's the next step?" asked Ellam.

"A conference. Is there somewhere we can all get together?"

"How many's all of us?"

"You, me, Mr. Bright, Strang, the divers, Doc. How many is that? Six or seven."

"My cabin might do. I'd suggest the crew messroom or the roughnecks' deck but we'd better leave them free for my lads and yours. They'll need somewhere to get out of the weather."

"Right you are. Your cabin it is. D'you think your cook could get some coffee and sandwiches?"

"I'd be surprised if he's not working on it already. Cooky likes crowds."

"Good. I'll get *Blackamoor* to send over some stores. This lot'll eat you out of house and home in a few hours."

"Don't worry, Commander. We keep plenty of food."

Five minutes later they were all collected in Ellam's cabin. With two sitting on the bunk, three on the settee, and Gaile and Ellam in the chairs the seven of them fitted in with room to spare. The cabin soon smelled of egg and bacon sandwiches and coffee.

Gaile waited till the food was finished. "Right, gentlemen, let's get down to business. We've located the hut and we're now refreshing the air. There are two men down there but only one is likely to be of much use to us. The other one has a broken leg. Once they've had time to recover, Doc, maybe you'll talk to them on the loudspeaker and see if you can suggest anything for the injured man."

The doctor nodded.

The commander turned to the divers. "Now let's hear what it's like down there."

"Well, sir, it's not easy to be sure. It's pretty dark down there but the hut seems to be almost level."

"Look at these plans. They might help you."

The men studied the drawings together then the senior diver spoke again. "Well, sir, it looks as if that deck there with the hut on it has collapsed. The main deck of the rig seems to be about twenty degrees to the bottom. But the hut's level so it must've collapsed at one end, there."

"Wreckage?"

"Lots of that, sir."

"Could you cut away enough debris to bring men up through?"

"Oh aye, sir. That shouldn't be too hard. There'd be a fair bit of cutting though. But how do we get them out of the hut, sir?"

"That's the problem," said Gaile. "Just let me recap." He made a sketch on a piece of paper. "That's about how it is, is that right?"

"Yes, sir."

"So the hut's level, just like it would be when the rig was upright." He added to his drawing. "So the outer door is there, like that."

"That's about it, sir."

The commander sat staring at the sketch.

"That space between the two doors would make a good escape chamber, sir," suggested Strang.

"That's what I was thinking. But how to do it."

"If we got them in there, sir, and flooded up, they'd still have a bit of air left at the top."

"True but it's far from ideal. That chamber's eight feet high. That means they'd have to have something in there to stand on to keep their heads above water. That could be done but remember one of them's got a broken leg. And it would all have to be done quickly and with no margin for errors. We'd have to break through to flood up.

These men aren't submariners, Strang. Just imagine what could happen with water pouring in there and them trying to keep their heads out. Then we have to get in and get them out. And with the flooding compressing that air, the CO_2 percentage would be near lethal. No, I don't like it."

"Commander," asked Bright. "Could you put me in the picture? I can't follow what you're trying to do. Don't you lower down some sort of diving bell, then just cut through into the hut and bring them out?"

"No, we don't, Mr. Bright. We don't have a diving bell like that. The Americans have one. They claim it works. We've never liked the idea."

"All right then. Why not cut the hut off in one piece and haul it up to the surface?"

"Too big a job, sir," said Strang. "It needs special lift ships. It's a salvage operation, not for saving lives in a hurry."

"Wait a minute, Lieutenant." It was Gaile. "You're right, of course, but Mr. Bright's given me an idea. Look here. If we can turn that hut over so that the outer door's facing down, then we could get the men into that compartment, shut the inside door, put in a bolt, blow the pressure up to four atmospheres, then the pressure would be equal inside and out. If the outer's door's then facing down, all that's needed is for the men inside to kick off the lugs and the door will fall open. The compartment would then be open to the sea but the pressure would hold the sea out. Then we put in a diver and take them out one at a time on free ascent up a shot rope. How's that?"

"That's just dandy, sir. But the door's not on the bottom. The way it is now . . ."

"I know that, Strang. That's the idea Mr. Bright gave me. First I thought of towing the rig over on its side but that's got too many dangers. It might go right over. Anything might happen. But look here at the drawings. If we cut free one side of that deck the hut's sitting on, then jack up that side of the deck and the hut with it, then the hut would turn through ninety degrees and bring that door facing down."

There was silence in the cabin. Everyone was staring at the drawings.

"That's a lot of cutting, Commander."

"Have you got a better idea?"

"No, sir. It's clever. It's brilliant. How do we jack it up to turn the hut over?"

"I've been thinking about that. What about getting *Blackamoor* to put a line down from the other side of the wreck and haul that deck over?"

"Could do, sir, but she's got a lot of power. It would take pretty careful timing."

"Mr. Strang, this whole bloody job's going to take careful timing."

Ellam spoke for the first time. "Can I say a word?"

"Of course, Captain."

"About hauling over this deck. I was wondering if we couldn't use one of *Circe*'s anchors. There's a lot of power in that windlass but it's easily controlled. If your divers cut one side of that deck free, fix chains to it, then shackle on to my anchor cable, we could heave the deck over that way. And being fixed to the anchor cable, the deck and the hut could be held just where you want it."

Gaile nodded slowly. "That's good, Captain. That's very good." He looked round the cabin and smiled grimly. "Well, gentlemen, we've got a plan. Now let's see if it works."

Chapter 10

Fresh air was a strange experience for Colney and Tucker. When the booming metallic voice from outside wakened them from their sleep towards death, they felt no urgency. Their poisoning had been slow and unspectacular. The voice was just another of the fantasies being woven by their oxygen starved brains. There was no physical distress. Rather the opposite, an overwhelming sense of peace and well-being. But that voice went on and on. It was harsh, commanding, insistent. It spoke their names. It dragged them back to reality. And reality was frightening.

Colney stirred and his brain began struggling with the jigsaw of memories. It was dark. He needed light. The emergency set. He stretched out and felt for it. Even that amount of movement sent a stab of pain through his lungs. He pressed the switch. Nothing. He stabbed it on and off, on and off. Nothing. Fear brought him wide awake. The set was dead. Fool, fool, fool. I left it on. I've been sleeping with the light on. Now I'm awake and it's dark. Terribly dark. What's that voice saying? Tap three repeat three times. Colney grabbed in the dark and found a piece of debris. He lashed out wildly. They'll never hear that. Have to get to the side of the hut. He started crawling. His arms and legs were like lead, pain grasped at his chest and he could hear his breath rasping in his throat. A cry and a curse. He was crawling the wrong way. He was on top of Tucker. He turned and scrambled away, hitting his head and legs on benches and unseen debris, ignoring the blows in his desperation to reach the bulkhead. Here it is. Three repeat three. He hammered. One, two, three. One, two, three. One, two, three. The voice boomed all round him. Five repeat five. It's just five they want. They said it was the Navy. That's the way they speak. Five repeat five means five. He hammered again, concentrating to sound the right number. The voice again. Air—they're going to give us air. Thank God. He listened then hammered back in reply.

He crouched there gasping for breath. There was cold sweat on his face. His body was racked with pain from his small exertions. Better do what they say. Better get back beside Tucker and lie down. Lord, it's so dark. "Tucker," he whispered hoarsely. "Tucker, where are you?"

"Over here. What's going on?" The words were slurred.

Colney felt his way over and collapsed beside the Texan. "They're going—going to give us—give us air," he gasped. He lay there trying to forget his pain, thinking of the air that was coming, saving his strength for that job he had to do, to uncap these bolts they were going to fire into the hut. How'll I find them? How'll I know where they are? Must get some sort of light. That torch. Where did I put it? He thought and a new fear gripped him. What if I can't find these bolts? What if they fire these bolts and I can't find them and they can't get the air in because I can't get the caps off? God. That torch. I tied it on to myself so I wouldn't lose it. He groped at his waist. There it is, inside my anorak. He pulled it out and flicked the switch. The light came on. He felt better. He relaxed and watched the beam swing round the hut as the torch swung loose in his hand. Have to switch it off. Must save it. Only light we've got now. Darkness again. It's not so frightening now. They're there outside and they're going to give us air. I can hear them now, tap, tap, tap. That voice again. Good, they're finding a place for the bolts. Hurry up, hurry up, I've not got much strength left.

The impact of the bolt gun sounded like a bomb hitting

the steel hut. As the noise eddied away, Colney started crawling along the hut. No, wait; two bolts, the voice said. Don't move till you're told. The wait seemed interminable. Then came the crash of the second bolt. Seconds, minutes, he had no idea of time. At last, the voice. Torch on, crawl forward, search. There they are, sticking through the shell, gleaming in the light. God, my chest, my arms, my legs, my head. I'll never make it. Tap three times if I could see the bolts, the voice said. One, two, three. Now unscrew them. God, where are my strong hands now? I can't move this one. Take a rest. Keep calm. Try the other one. Hallelujah, it moved. The cap spun the rest of the way easily and came off in his hand. One off and one to go. Easy does it. Take another rest. Now try that first one again. Come on, give all you've got, Ted Colney. There you are, it moved. Keep turning, turning. Off. He fell against the bulkhead, panting and clutching at his chest. Where's that fresh air? He listened.

He had expected it to come with a hiss and a rush. There was no sound other than the foul air rasping in his own throat. He put his hands over the uncapped bolts. Nothing. Then he remembered. Tap when both bolt heads are off. How many times was it? Four? No, five. He hammered five times, then waited. It was scarcely audible at first, just a faint rustle like wind-stirred leaves. Then suddenly it burst through with a great swoosh like a Guy Fawkes rocket soaring skywards. He lay where he was, exhausted, feeling the air fanning across him and the tears flooding down his cheeks.

It was not till his hysteria had subsided and he had crawled back to the bunk where Tucker was lying that he noticed the smell. It was a smell of staleness, vaguely offensive, disappointing after the hope of freshness. For a few moments Colney was gripped by panic. They had made a mistake up there on the surface. It wasn't fresh air they were pumping in. It was some sort of gas. Someone had connected the wrong cylinder. No, that can't be right. I feel better. It must be air or some special mixture to revive us. That's it. There's a chemical scent to it. Then he realised what was happening and he started to laugh. It hurt his chest to laugh but he could not stop himself.

"What's up with you?" growled Tucker.

"It's—it's that smell. It was worrying me. It—it doesn't smell like fresh air, does it."

"What's fresh air smell like? Who cares? I feel better."

"So do I but the smell worried me. Not now though. D'you know what it is?"

"No I don't. But go on, tell me. Share the joke."

"It's us, Tucker. The smell is us. That stale smell is you and me, and that smell of chemicals is just the lab. Don't you see? We'd lost our sense of smell. Now we're getting it back. That's why we smell these smells. We'd lost our sense of smell with all that CO_2."

The Texan grunted. "Very scientific, I'm sure. Now put on the light so I can see what fresh air looks like."

Colney's laughter stopped abruptly. "There is no light," he said quietly. "The emergency set's dead."

"Hell. It helped having that light."

"I'm sorry, Tucker."

"Why be sorry? It's not your fault."

"It is, you know. I must have left it on when we dozed off. I hate the dark, you see. I'm sorry."

"Quit being so sorry, will you, Limey. It won't be for long now. They'll have us out of here in no time."

"I hope so. How's that leg of yours?"

"It'll do. It'll have to. Mind you, that air maybe clears your head but it sure makes me feel this busted pin."

"There's some aspirin in that first-aid kit. Will I get it?"

Tucker chuckled. "I'll pass the aspirin. If you've got a bottle of bourbon, that might help."

"What's that funny saying again? If we had some

whisky we could have whisky and water, if we had some water. There is some water, Tucker. Do you want some?"

"Yeah, I'll take some. I'll tell myself it's bourbon. Mind over matter. They say it works."

Colney shone the torch and poured a drink for the big man who propped himself up and rolled it round his mouth before swallowing it down.

"Just what I thought, Limey. Mind over matter. It's a load of crap."

Colney smiled and took some water himself. There was not much left in the jar; maybe a cup each.

For the next half-hour they lay still, not talking, savouring the air and their restored sense of smell, all the time breathing deeply to expel every last vestige of the poison from their lungs. There were sounds from outside to comfort them, sounds of the divers moving on and around the hut, metallic sounds as wreckage was cut free and dragged away to clear a space for Gaile's rescue plan. But the noise which meant most to them was the hiss of the air pouring into the hut.

When it stopped it was as if a thong had tightened round their throats. They said nothing. There were still sounds from outside but they seemed more remote than before. They lay in the blackness of the hut, listening for the sound of the air, trying not to think of what might have happened. Then it came back, suddenly, noisily, and they relaxed. The voice boomed through from outside. "Sorry about that, chaps. We were switching bottles. Somebody boobed. It won't happen again."

Tucker was the first to speak. "Thank God for that. Gave me quite a turn."

"Yes," said Colney. "It's interesting how quickly one learns to rely on something. That's how brainwashing works, isn't it. Give a man something then take it away for no reason. Give him it back and tell him it's never been missing. No wonder people soon get confused."

"Yeah, but we've come up with a new angle. Don't

they usually keep the lights on all the time? They should try the dark. They should try the dark down here at the bottom of the sea."

Colney nodded, unseen. He thought he sensed a trace of panic in Tucker's voice. He was relieved. He had thought the Texan was immune to the strain. He felt more on a level with him now. "Yes, I'm sorry about the light."

"For crissake, Limey, shut up being sorry. It's done and that's that. Is there anything to eat?"

"Sor—no, I mustn't say that, must I. No, there's nothing left to eat."

"Hell, I'm hungry. I just hope there's some decent grub waiting for us up there. How's your Navy for food, Colney?"

"I've no idea. It couldn't be any worse than the Army."

"How d'you know about the Army?"

"I wasted the war in it. No, that's not true. I spent most of the time making maps and doing surveys. It was quite interesting. But the food wasn't up to much."

"You're a queer cuss. You keep surprising me. First I discover you're married. Now you tell me you were in the war."

"Everyone was in the war, Tucker. Weren't you?"

"Sure I was in it. I was in construction. It was a funny outfit, sort of half civilian half Navy. We built airfields, ports, that sort of thing. The food there was good. By God, it was good. That was the first thing we always built; our own cookhouse."

"Maybe we shouldn't talk about food when we haven't got any."

"Why not? We got time on our hands. Don't you like food or something?"

"Yes, I like a nice meal now and again. Most of the time I seem to be too busy to bother much."

"I've noticed. You're missing something, Colney. No, maybe not with this English cooking. God, that Brown

Windsor soup and that soaking wet cabbage. I hope that's not what we're going to get when we get out of here."

"It's more than likely."

Tucker groaned in the darkness. "All the more reason to think about real food. I'll tell you what. I'll tell you what I'd like right now. I'd like clam chowder, thick, steaming hot. Then a T-bone steak, rare, with some salad on the side. To finish off I'll have apple pie *à la mode*. Oh, and a barrel of coffee to wash it all down. And while it's all cooking, I'll have a couple of hot dogs with lots of mustard, and three or four bourbons on the rocks. How's that?"

"I'm afraid it sounds quite bilious to me."

"All right, so it's your turn. What's your order?"

"Well, if I must, I think I'll start with a dry sherry, then some potted shrimps. An *escalope* of veal, a few chips and French beans, a glass of hock, then some cheese."

"It's not my style, Colney, but I'd settle for it right now. God, I'm hungry."

"I'm not surprised. I told you not to talk about food. Even I feel a bit peckish now."

"Good. That makes two of us. We gotta talk about something."

"If you say so."

"What's the matter with you, Limey? Aren't you pleased at getting your breath back? Aren't you thinking about what you're going to do when you get out of here?"

"Not really. That seems too remote and anyway I'll just go on doing what I've always done. What I am thinking about is how they're going to get us out. It's an interesting problem. I should be able to work it out from first principles."

"Why bother?" asked Tucker. "Your Navy's up there. They're the experts. Leave it to them. I'll tell you what I'm thinking about, Colney. I'm thinking about things that make me forget my leg, and the cold, and the dark. I'm thinking about a hot shower. No, not a shower, a bath. A huge boiling hot bath like the ones you get in Japan. You ever been to Japan, Colney?"

"No."

"You've missed something, man. They're a queer bunch, mind you, always bowing and sucking their teeth, but they know a thing or two. They sure know about baths. Y'see, how it is is like this. You get stripped off and squat down on a wooden stool. Then a smart little piece comes in and flings a bucket of water over you, then scrubs you all over with soap and flings some more water on you. Then you get into the bath, after you're all clean, y'see. And this bath's boiling hot. It's deep and there's maybe half a dozen of you in it together. There's a fire going all the time underneath to keep it hot. You're in this water up to your neck and it's hot, hot, hot, man. It sort of cooks you. All your aches and pains are cooked right out of you. Soon you haven't a care in the world. When you get out of there you're like a well done lobster. They steer you on to a table and then the massage starts. Now that's real painful. They use old blind women and they've got fingers like steel claws. Man, they can make you scream. But it's great when it's all over. You feel like you've been taken to bits, each part cleaned and oiled, and all put together again like new. That's what I'm thinking about, Colney."

"It sounds rather dreadful. And very public."

Brad chuckled. "I guess it does to you. But you can have private baths too. They're even better. Cost more but you get value. There they don't use old blind women; no, sir. And the massage is sort of different, if you know what I mean."

"I can imagine."

"I can imagine," mimicked Tucker. "Hell, you Limeys are all the same. You don't fool me though. I remember an old bag in Venezuela. She knew all about Limeys. Yanks too for that matter. D'you know what she used to say?"

"No."

"She used to say Limeys are nice and polite till the bedroom door's shut. Then they go at you like mad bulls."

"And what did she have to say about Americans?"

"Hell, that was smart too. She said most Yanks want to fall in love with their whores."

"How very astute of her. Don't you think the English system has a lot to commend it?"

The Texan laughed and the sound echoed eerily in the blackness. "I guess you're right. I guess I use the English system but I don't keep it a secret."

"You miss the point, Tucker. The system isn't English unless you keep it secret."

"Aw, balls, man. You're all theory and no action. What d'you know about women?"

"Very little, I suppose. About Japanese or Venezuelan professionals, nothing at all. I can't say I feel I've missed much."

"Well, I guess what you've never had you don't miss. By God, I sure miss it right now." He paused. "Mind you, I don't class all Limeys the same. Take that youngster who's skipper of *Circe*. Johnny Ellam. There's one after my own heart. D'you know him?"

"*Circe*? Ellam? Should I know them?"

"You should but you probably don't. You've probably forgotten there's anything outside this bloody lab of yours. *Circe*, the workboat. Ellam's her skipper."

"Oh, yes. No, I don't think I know him."

"You soon will. I'll bet he's up there right now with the Navy, waiting for us to come out. He's a Limey I like. None of this fancy talk, right down to earth, tough as they come, and always ready for a bit of fun. Yes, sir; that's a man I like. And the rig crew, they were a good bunch. I hope they got off."

"You seem to like a lot of Limeys."

"I suppose I do at that. I like most people."

"Why do you dislike me then?"

"Who said I didn't like you? I just don't know what makes you tick. And I don't like the way you talk, like you was God or something."

"What an odd comparison."

"Well, you know what I mean. 'I'm the great genius and you're just a big bum of a driller from Texas.' That sort of thing."

"I never said that," snapped Colney.

"Sure, you never said it. But you meant it. You and your theories about rocks. I've been making hole for forty years. I've picked up a thing or two about rocks."

"I'm sure you have. But I've never discussed my theories with you."

"Of course not. I'm too dumb for your theories. I just cut cores and you send all your secret reports to Brightboy in London."

"That's the way Roger wanted it. He knows what he's doing. He's got a big job. And he got it on merit."

"So they say. All right, so he's smart. He knows his oil business. He's tough, he's smooth. Christ, he's smooth. I tell you, Bright's a Limey I really don't like."

"Now we're getting somewhere. What's wrong with Roger?"

"What's right with him? He talks like he's got a pebble under his tongue, he knows just what to say and how to say it, and he'd strangle his grandmother for a nickel."

"That doesn't sound like the Roger Bright I know."

"You wait, Colney. I've seen them come and go. You're his blue-eyed boy now. But just wait. One of these days he'll get tired of all your dry holes. He'll hear rumbles that New York's tired waiting. Then you'll be looking for a new oil company."

"I won't complain. If I don't find what I'm looking for, why should I?"

"O.K. Have it your way. You'll remember me when it happens. I'm no egghead, Colney, but I know people like I know oil wells. And that's some."

The voice from outside boomed all around them.

"Speak of the devil," said Tucker.

The voice was introducing itself as Roger Bright. As he sat in the dark, listening, Ted Colney was thinking that Tucker was talking a lot more than usual. Talk like that from a man like that could mean he was afraid. That kind of fear in a man as tough as Brad Tucker was itself frightening.

Chapter 11

"Hallo there, Ted. Hallo, Brad. Roger Bright here. Are you feeling better with some fresh air in your lungs? No, don't try to answer. The doctor up here says all the CO_2's gone from the hut. We're getting pure air back through the exhaust now." The voice was distorted through the microphone and the speaker, the water and the steel shell, but to anyone who knew him it was unmistakably Roger who was talking. The polished accent was marred but the way the words were strung together, the way the emphasis was laid and lifted, was like a signature. "How's that leg, Brad? Don't you worry. The doctor will speak in just a moment. He'll be able to tell you how to save it till you get back up here. That should not be too long. The Navy's here in force. Commander Gaile has it all worked out. He'll have you out of there before you can say Inoco. By the way, Brad, Johnny Ellam sends his regards. He says he hopes it's either your right or left leg that's broken."

"What'd I tell you," burst out Tucker. "Johnny's up there. I told you, didn't I. He's up there now, still making with the jokes." His laughter was silenced by the voice.

"Ted, how about you? You're not injured so you're the one who's going to have to do what's needed from inside when the time comes. We'll be giving you instructions later on. For now just do what the doctor says, take it easy, rest up. I almost forgot, Ted. There's a message for you. I just got it through from London. Carol's been on the phone to the office. She sends her love. From the children too. She says to hurry up and come home. That goes for me too, Ted. I'm waiting for that good news on that last core. Keep your chins up, both of you. Here's the doctor now."

There was a tightness in Colney's throat. That's Carol for sure. I suppose I'm in the headlines. She wouldn't miss a headline. No, that's not fair. She's tried. Too much, I suppose. But maybe that was my fault.

> *Ding dong dell*
> *Teddy's down the well*
> *Who pushed him in?*
> *Little Carol Colney. Or did he jump?*

He shook his head. It doesn't even rhyme.

The doctor's voice was flatter, less distinctive. It blared instructions on what to do with Tucker's broken leg. Do not move it. If possible splint it. If there is a wound, cover it with a clean piece of cloth. It had all been done. Then the voice gave advice on how to conserve their strength. Try and keep warm. Don't move about. Exercise where you are with arm and leg and body movements. Rest. Keep cheerful. Tap three times if you have recovered enough to understand these instructions.

Tucker had to shout at Colney to go and tap on the bulkhead. Ted had been listening to the doctor with only half his mind. He crawled over and hammered the acknowledgment. He was still thinking of his wife and her unexpected message.

Tucker was talking again. "It's all right for that bloody doctor. Keep warm. Keep cheerful. Do your daily dozen. Don't move about. What the hell's he think we're going to do? Play ball?"

"He's only trying to help. He probably just wanted to reassure us."

"It's all right for you, Colney. Love from your wife and kids. Sweet talk from Brightboy."

"You seemed to get your share. You were laughing a few minutes ago."

"Yeah, thank God for Johnny Ellam. At least he wants

to see us up there alive. Not just me, you too. That's his type. He's normal. He likes people. Not like that bastard Bright. He let the cat out of the bag. D'you notice?"

"Which cat? I don't understand."

"No wonder he likes you, Limey. He could con the pants off you any day. The cat about the last core, of course. That's why he wants us up. Not for us. Not likely. For what we can tell him about that core."

"I wouldn't say that. Of course he wants to know about that core. You know about these Dutch options as well as I do. They expire soon. Roger's got to decide about them. He wants evidence. So would you."

"Yeah, and I'd want better evidence than you've got. Theory's all right but it's facts that matter. And the fact is that this was another dry hole."

"True, as far as we went down. But that's nothing. I don't need a show of oil or gas to tell me what's down there. Roger's right. That last core could be very important."

"Sure it could. Once he knows there's nothing there he'll cancel the options and save a lot of cash. But thank God we can't tell him from down here."

"Why not? Maybe we should. Maybe if I shout loud over near the side, they'll pick it up."

"I'll tell you why not, Colney. Because when Brightboy hears from you he'll lose interest in getting us up out of here."

"That's nonsense."

"Is it? You just wait. That was him just warming up. He'll be back on the line soon saying time's short and could you give him some sort of sign. I know them all, Colney. I've seen it all before. I remember one just like Brightboy. He's not so special. No one's special if you can see through them."

Colney said nothing. He was not interested in Tucker's theories. He had been reminded of his own theory and he was clinging to that memory to dispel that other memory of his wife. He realised that for eighteen hours he had forgotten about his theory of unique structures. For months he had thought of little else; now he packed his brain with all the details.

It had started when Roger Bright brought him home from the Persian Gulf to join the North Sea team. Ted's first report on the seismic survey followed a pattern many geologists supported. The coal measures off the East Coast of England, stretching across almost in a straight line to the huge Dutch gas field at Groningen, were probably feeding methane up into the sand layers. It was generally agreed that the North Sea basin offered good chances of gas. The prospects for oil were less rosy. Gas was not what Bright wanted but he was too shrewd not to hedge his bets. He offered for and got rights on blocks along and on either side of that line. He had no rig at that time; Offshore Five was being hauled half-way round the world to be refitted for the North Sea. He was happy to let his competitors rush in and start test drilling on their own blocks. Their results would prove or disprove the presence of gas in commercial quantities. Bright went ahead building the Yarmouth base, pushing the shipyards to hurry on the new rigs, gathering the best brains he could find into the Inoco fold. And while he waited for Offshore Five he set Ted Colney the task of finding an area where there might be oil. Now Colney was sure he had found it.

His unique structure theory had come from his fascination with the vast salt deposits stretching out under the sea bed from the north of the continent. The salt had come from the evaporation of the so-called Zechstein Sea in upper-Permian times. It was thousands of feet thick and the pressures and disturbances of millions of years had folded it, creased it, billowed and ballooned it into its present complex of ridges and domes. Oilmen knew about salt domes. Round the edges of the mushroom shaped structures they had found oil traps. They had been of the usual type, reservoir rocks holding oil as a sponge holds water, the area sealed in by an impermeable layer. Traps like that would not likely be commercial in the North Sea where the breakeven figure was a reserve of five hundred thousand million barrels. Colney's theory came from a new reading of the seismic data. He flung aside all the usual assumptions. He posed the question: What if the reflecting layer under the salt is not what we assume it to be? And the exciting answer to that was that the seismic data must then mean that the waves returning through the salt domes were not only travelling through salt but also through liquid. And the liquid could not be brine for the waves suggested a viscosity which could only mean oil. Liquid oil. Huge caverns of liquid oil.

No oilman would believe it. Only the man in the street believed that oil lay in pools under the ground. Oilmen knew that oil lay in reservoir rocks. Colney accepted this. His oil had come from reservoir rocks. But it was no longer in them. His theory of unique structure was that when the earth's crust heaved and twisted and the salt layer was creased and ballooned, it did not billow up into solid domes. First the crust of the domes grew, then succeeding disturbances pushed and pulled at more of the layer, creating caverns inside the first crust. Much later, new strains fractured the reservoir rocks round the edges of the domes, and the pressure outside and the vacuum inside pushed and sucked the oil from the rocks into the domes. Then the next folding rejoined the salt crust to seal the oil inside.

At first it had only been an idea. But the more he studied it, the more convinced he was that he was right. Only drilling would prove it finally. He had gone back to Roger Bright. He had told him that he had found a series of unique structures which could contain oil in quantity. At least ten times the commercial minimum. Bright had only asked where the area was. Roger's great talent was in picking the right men then trusting them. He had known Ted Colney long enough to know he would give no details till he was quite certain. Certainty to him meant oil at the well-head.

The area was the whole northern part of the Dutch sector, running just over the border into the British sector on Dogger Bank. The timing could not have been better. The Dutch area was out of the question because of the withdrawal of all permits pending final legislation. But the argument about the dividing line between the Dutch and British areas had just been settled. The British blocks on the median line were on offer. Roger got the ones he wanted. Offshore Five was ready to go on site.

That was more than six months ago, three and a bit holes ago. They had all been dry and Inoco's competitors sighed with relief. Everyone said Colney was mad; everyone said Bright was mad to let a madman have his head. All they knew was that Offshore Five was drilling in positions they thought to be useless. Their relief was because this time they seemed to be right. They had underestimated Colney and Bright before. If this last hole had gone down another few hundred feet the headlines in the papers might have been different. Colney was sure he was within that distance of the first of his underground treasure houses.

No one, not even Bright, yet knew the details of his theory. Bright, his assistant Harry Ashton, and the Dutchman van Sluys knew he was working on the idea of a unique structure. That was all they knew. Bright had never said anything to discourage him. Even the dry holes had not shaken his faith. Colney knew the others were sceptical. Now that rescue was near, that scepticism would be short lived. They could clear away the wreckage of Offshore Five, bring in a new rig, fish out the drill pipe from this hole and pierce the last few hundred feet to the oil he was sure was there. Even if they could not clear this hole, the Dutch options would let them move into the really wealthy area. All the work to date had convinced Ted that his theory was right. He had made only one big mistake. The reserves of oil were not ten times but at least fifty times the commercial minimum of five hundred thousand million barrels. It was going to be one of the biggest strikes of all time.

Thinking again of his theory, Colney was filled with a new enthusiasm to be out of the hut and back on the surface. He had managed to rid his mind of any thought of his wife. He was at peace with the only thing that had ever brought him lasting satisfaction, his work. The utter blackness of the hut, without shape or shadow to relieve it, did not frighten him at all now. The sounds barely filtered through to him; the hissing air, the muted clatter of the rescue work outside, the constant drawl of Tucker's voice. He heard bits of what the Texan was saying but he heard as an eavesdropper not as someone in conversation. Now and again the drawl stopped, only to start up again on some new reminiscence. That was what Brad was doing, clawing back through a long full life for things to talk about. As if talking was a lifeline he dare not let go of.

Brad Tucker had worked on almost every major oil field in the world. First ashore, then when offshore drilling started, on every type of rig. He knew all the famous names from the oil fields. The wildcatters, the explosives men who doused the well-head fires, the poor farmers become millionaires overnight, the oil lease pedlars, the charlatans and gamblers who reaped a rich reward from thrill hungry roughnecks, the Britishers gone native in the Persian Gulf, the Americans blowing themselves to smithereens making forbidden alcohol in Arabia. He knew them all and he talked of them all. The stories had no pattern, no common characters. They tumbled out in a mad torrent. There were stories of pimps and prostitutes, parties, orgies, gushers, disasters. Women and liquor were recurrent themes. They were Brad's vices but he looked back on them as the high points in a life of sweat, blood and blisters. They were his recreations and he talked of them with the same pride as other men talk of gardens or golf. But he talked too of oil wells. He talked of his drilling as a cabinet-maker talks of his craft, as an artist talks of his work. He spoke of his wells with a gentleness, almost a reverence, which was absent when he spoke of his women. Oil wells had a sort of permanence, a beauty only understood by those who gave their lives to the business of fashioning them. To Brad a landscape was not complete without a forest of derricks and a herd of jack pumps nodding their heads as they sucked their treacly meal up out of the depths. His seascapes too had to have huge steel islands rearing up out of the water and schools of tugs and barges and tankers leaping the waves. Brad Tucker was as dedicated to the oil business as Ted Colney was to his rocks.

The geologist started listening. He understood dedication and his respect for the Texan grew as the voice drawled on. But he noticed other things. The drawl was faster than usual, pitched higher. The voice fumbled with simple words, rasped with a new harshness, fell silent sometimes to be replaced by a feverish gasping. Then it would start up again, drawling, talking, remembering, gasping. Ted noticed something else. It was a new smell. It was cloying, sweetish, offensive. It made his empty stomach heave. It was a smell he knew. For minutes he could not place it. Then he remembered. In the Army, in Normandy after the invasion. It was the smell of rotting flesh.

Tucker's leg's going bad on him. What can I do? He mustn't get to know. I'll tell them to hurry up. I'll tell them Tucker's in bad shape. But he'll hear me if I shout. I can't do that. What good would it do anyway? They'll be hurrying as fast as they can. God, what can I do?

As if in answer the voice from outside boomed round the hut. Every half-hour since Roger Bright had spoken, the voice had talked. It had told them what was going on, assured them that everything was all right, asked them for an acknowledgment that they were still in touch. Colney flashed the torch to check his watch. Even that dim light was almost blinding. That's funny. It's only twenty minutes since the last time. Six o'clock it was. Now it's twenty past. It's been each half-hour. Somebody's read the clock wrong up there. Damned fools. The voice soon put him right.

"Hallo there, Mr. Colney. Hallo there, Mr. Tucker. This is Commander Gaile here. We've gone as far as we can go for the moment. It'll soon be dark and the weather up here's getting a bit dirty. We can't bring you up in the dark anyway so we're packing up for the night. You've got plenty of fresh air down there now so we're going to cut off the supply. We'll be in touch again first thing in the morning. Mr. Colney, you're the one who can move about. Would you go to the inlet and exhaust pipes and screw the caps back on them. I'm shutting off the air now. Tap four times, please, when the caps are on."

The voice cut off and the only sound was the hissing air. Then it petered out and a dreadful silence filled the hut.

Colney was afraid but he started crawling through the darkness in answer to the orders.

"What's going on?" demanded Tucker, the words slurred with his fever. "Why's the air stopped? What're these bastards doing up there? They said that wouldn't happen again."

"Didn't you hear?" shouted Colney. "They just told us. It's getting dark and the weather's bad. They're shutting off the air till the morning. I've got to cap these pipes."

"Like hell you will. Stay where you are. Where are you, you stupid Limey? Don't cap them, Colney. Don't you see. They're giving up. They're leaving us to die."

"Shut up, Tucker. We'll be all right." Colney crawled on and flashed the torch to find the pipes.

"Don't do it, Colney. For crissake, don't do it. It's that bastard Bright. You've told him, haven't you. You've told him about that core. I must've been asleep and you've told him. Now he's leaving us. I knew he would. I told you." The Texan's voice was shrill and crazed.

Colney was feeling about the deck for the caps. Where the

devil did I put them? He tried to shut out the sound of Tucker's raving. Bits of debris were crashing all round the inside of the hut as Tucker threw everything he could lay his hands on.

"Don't do it, Colney. I'll kill you, you bastard. Where are you?"

Not where am I. Where are these damned caps? Think. Think. What did I do with them?

Gaile's voice came back from outside. "What's going on down there? We're getting a lot of noise in the listening gear. Colney, this is urgent. We must unmoor at once. Tap three times if you heard my message." Colney felt around desperately for something to hammer back with. He knew what could happen. If the hoses outside were torn off the sea would pour in through the bolts. His hand felt something hard in the pocket of his anorak. It was one of the caps. Other pocket. Thank God. Both of them. Tap three times to say I heard the message. Tap—tap— tap. Now where are these bolts? There, that's one. Turn the cap back half a turn to set the thread. Good. It spun on easily and he screwed it up tight. Now the other one.

Gaile's voice boomed again. "We heard three taps. Give four repeat four when both caps are on."

All right, all right. Keep your hair on. I'm doing my best. You put me off just now. Tucker too was trying to put him off. The cap went on. One, two, three, four.

"Thank you, Mr. Colney. We're disconnecting now. Don't worry. You'll be all right. We'll be back down there at daylight. Good luck."

"Bastards," roared Tucker. And he went on shouting it till he slipped off the bunk, screamed as the rotting wound on his leg slammed down on the deck, and he passed out.

Chapter 12

Frank Gaile's bit of dirty weather was already a moderate gale from the north-west. He had ignored the signs all afternoon; the falling barometer, the warnings on the radio, the suspicious lull in the stiff breeze about four o'clock, then the quick backing of the wind. He had ignored the signs because he wanted to do as much as he could down below. The official limit for diving was Force 5. He and the divers were happy enough with a bit more wind and sea than that. But now it was Force 7 and rising. He was glad he had decided to call a halt. The men and equipment were back on board. *Circe*'s decks were swilling with water as she rolled at her moorings with the wind and sea roaring across her from the port beam.

The commander hauled open the lee door of the wheelhouse and grabbed for support as a wave crashed on board and the workboat heeled over. His oilskins were streaming water and his wet hair straggled down over his brow. "Take her away, Captain," he yelled.

Ellam was standing at the centre window, steadying himself with a hand on the pilot chair. He waved and spoke into the loud-hailer. "Slack away aft. And easy does it. Don't let it run." He waited for the roll to port then walked the few steps up the sloping deck to the starboard door. He helped Gaile inside then went out to the wing of the bridge. The men at the stern had heard. They were slacking down the wire which held *Circe* broadside to the rising gale. The deck aft was flooding and draining with each wave, the men slipping on the wet deck, grabbing for handholds, water sloshing up round their thighs, receding then welling up again. There were Navy men down there helping *Circe*'s crew. The mass of rescue gear was already stowed below or lashed in place on deck. The lengthening flight of wire let the workboat's stern drift downwind. The wind and sea came round the port bow. The rolling changed to a sickening corkscrew motion. The men were looking up at Ellam. They were at the end of the wire. The young captain watched, judging his moment. One man was holding the brightly coloured buoy over the stern rail, the buoy to mark where the wire and the anchor lay on the bottom. The ship rolled and twisted, the wire heaved up out of the sea, taut as a bowstring. *Circe* rolled back slowly and the wire sagged out of sight. "Let go," yelled Ellam, upping both arms high in case the wind whipped his words away unheard. The men sprang back, the wire slid through the bitts, snapping its end viciously as it disappeared, the buoy splashed into the water, and *Circe* quickly swung her stern away and faced up to the gale, bow on.

Ellam went back into the wheelhouse and set the engines to Slow Ahead. He felt rather than heard the answering beat of the diesels. The little ship rode easier with the sea ahead. She was pitching now, showering spray over the men huddled in the bows and rattling it against the bridge windows. The motors on the clear view screens whined as they whirled the glass discs, throwing away the water. Ellam peered for'ard. The cloud had been well broken but now an overcast was sweeping in from the north-west to bring an early dusk. He switched on a floodlight on the front of the bridge. The light picked out and reflected from every drop of flying spray. It looked like a freak snow storm. The bosun signalled from the bow. *Circe* had come ahead enough to slack down the doubled rope holding the bow to the wreck of Offshore Five.

Johnny turned up the volume on the hailer. "Let go."

He saw the men bend to throw off one end of the rope. It slipped through the fairlead and was gone. The bosun had the other end on the turning drum of the windlass. Ellam breathed out. So far so good. According to plan but it's not over yet. Plans are fine but gales are fickle. Bloody fool, that commander, waiting so long. We'll be lucky if we don't lose someone overboard. He stopped the engines and signed to the man at the wheel to hold her up. It had all been rehearsed. The bosun knew what to do. The men should be safe. Lifelines were stretched, they were all hooked on, and they all had lifejackets. But the sea was already higher than Johnny liked. *Circe* was dipping her bow in now, She was shipping solid water. The men were fighting to hold their feet. Must be that rope holding her head down. Half Ahead. Two more waves grinning hungrily over the bow but only slopping their crests on board. That's better. She's easier now. That bosun's a wonder. That rope's coming in fast. Just the eye to come clear of the wreck and we're home and dry. Well, wet but out of trouble.

He stopped the engines again and peered down at the bow. The rope was rolling in round the drum, back and down through the manhole into the locker. Remember that, pump that locker. Must be a lot of water down there now. Damn. The coils of rope were skidding on the drum. The rope was stretching out taut over the water. Hold on, lads. It'll pull clear of the wreck. It must. But the snagged rope held and *Circe*'s bow dug into the next wave. The water came on board grey-green and edged with foam. The ship shuddered with the impact and, as the wave broke and spewed aft in a swirling torrent, Ellam saw his men being hurled about like corks in a mill-race. Christ.

The water was already clearing. There was one figure slumped over the still turning drum of the windlass. As Ellam watched, the man moved, dragging himself upright and grabbing at the mooring rope. Thank God. That's that bloody bosun. Take more than a sea to finish him off. The other three were down on the tiny foredeck, two spreadeagled, one sitting up shaking his head. Their lifelines were still hooked on. Men from aft were down there, lifting their mates, unhooking them, helping them off the deck. Up in the bows the bosun was struggling alone with the rope. There was no sign of it ahead. It had come clear or parted.

"Come on then," yelled Johnny down to the deck. "What the hell're you thinking of? Get up for'ard and get that rope in." He had the engines at Slow Ahead, stemming the sea.

Two of the men looked up, their faces showing white in the floodlight, then ran up to the bows. In five minutes the rope was on board and stowed, the manhole of the locker sealed, and everyone off the decks. Ellam backed his ship carefully down wind, clear of the area of the wreck. He concentrated on the job, trying to stifle his anger, trying not to think of how badly injured these men were. *Circe*, free and unfettered, was riding the sea easily, pitching and rearing, occasionally lifting water over her bow and down along her decks, but always shaking it off to face the next wave. She had been built to take it rough. The wind was still rising but it sounded like the baying and whining of hounds cheated of the kill.

Gaile leaned on the bridgefront beside Ellam. "That was a fine piece of shiphandling, Captain."

"Sure," snapped Johnny. "Bloody fine it was. Almost washed half my crew overboard. God knows how badly hurt they are."

"They walked away from it. They'll be all right. It was just one of those things. It wasn't your fault."

"It happened, didn't it. It has to be someone's fault. It's my ship. I was up here so it's my fault."

"It's me who's really to blame. I kept you moored too long. I'm sorry about that."

"Too bloody late to be sorry now."

"Don't worry, Captain. The doctor's on board. He'll look after them."

"That makes it all right then, does it. The Navy's

here and all that cock. So never mind the split heads and the broken bones."

Gaile had had enough. "All right, Ellam. So it was your fault. You were too bloody mean to lose a rope. You should've cut it as soon as you were head to sea. Is that what you wanted to hear?"

Johnny turned his eyes away from the heaving bow and glared at the commander. The phone buzzed. He unhooked it and listened. "Thanks." He put the phone back in place and grinned at Gaile. "That's what I wanted to hear, Commander. Two cracked ribs and a sprained ankle." He turned back to watch the angry sea. "And I didn't lose that rope."

It was Gaile's turn to smile. He felt at home with this reckless, foul-mouthed, quick-tempered, capable young man. He settled himself more comfortably against the front of the wheelhouse, arms on the window ledge, face close to the glass, feet splayed on the rubber matting. He felt at home there on the bridge of a ship again, in the North Sea with a storm force wind howling outside, his body moving naturally against the movement of ship and sea. This was where Frank Gaile belonged; not sitting at a desk or parading the dais in a lecture room. That's fine, he told himself. All good kids' stuff. Man against nature, and winning. But what about that other fight, the one I'm out here to win. Man against the deep, man against time. Will I win that?

He peered out into the gloom. *Blackamoor* was hove to a mile to the north, her shape showing intermittently as a curtain of spray shut then sagged open around her. It had been a hectic afternoon for everyone. The frigate's crew had been out laying wreck buoys round the site. The cutters had chugged ceaselessly between *Circe* and *Blackamoor*, taking back empty cylinders for refilling, returning them full to the workboat. The divers had worked nonstop cutting away the mass of tangled steel on top of the geology hut and surveying the crumpled deck on which the hut stood to find the best way of getting that door facing down to turn it into an escape hatch. It was slow, tedious work. The lights were little use down there in the tide-stirred murk. The men had to rely on touch and instinct. It had soon been clear that there was not enough cutting gas to finish the job. Bright had called Yarmouth base and in an hour and a half the big helicopter was hovering over the site, dangling fresh bottles down on to *Circe's* deck. The gas arrived just after the lull in the weather. Now there was enough gas to finish the job but was there enough time? Less than three hours of daylight.

Then the wind backed and the barometer plummeted. Daylight was no longer the controlling factor. The weather had taken over. Gaile knew from that moment that any slight hope of getting Tucker and Colney out that day had gone. Darkness was always a problem. No one liked diving in the dark. But if the weather had held, or even better slacked up to give smooth sea conditions, the divers would have worked on into the night to get the men out. Now there was no hope. The sea was going to be too rough. The men had worked on down below far past the official safety limit. They had got all the debris cleared away from the top of the hut. One more hour, two at the most could have seen the job done. But there were no hours, barely minutes to get the air cut off, the men and gear on board, and *Circe* off the site. That had been touch and go. Ellam had said nothing, watching the storm build, waiting till everything was secured. Gaile had known the young man must be worried. He would have been himself. She was a tough little ship but staying moored broadside to this kind of sea would test the best hull. But that was over, thank God. Hove to like this, they could ride out the worst the Dogger Bank could offer. There were only two problems now. How long would the storm last? And how would his rescue plan work if he got the chance to try it? There was another question. What about that noise in the hut the Sonar man reported just before they disconnected? It had been like a fight, screaming and things being thrown. What had happened down inside that hut?

He was sure his plan was a good one, the only one. It would succeed if . . . There were so many "ifs." If the weather eased in time to get back over the wreck before the air ran out. That was a fair chance. He had enriched the air for the last hour before cutting it off. They would be lying still down there, maybe sleeping; that would save a bit. But it must be hellish cold. So they would be breathing faster. That would use more again. Say eighteen hours. Noon to-morrow. That was the "if" he had to ignore. There were plenty others. If the hut held up against the pressure of the water for another night. If the two men understood his instructions and made no mistakes. If the calculations he had made from his cardboard mockup in the afternoon were right. If the storm did not move the rig. If every order was given correctly, at the right time, and was obeyed instantly. If, if, if.

The commander pulled his face back from the window as *Circe* pounded down on top of a huge wave and the impact shuddered through every inch of her and into and through every muscle of every man on board. That's quite a storm, he decided. Even if the wind drops, how long will that sea last afterwards? He shrugged himself down on to the window ledge. He wondered what his wife and two boys would be thinking. He had had no time to phone from the Clyde. But he knew they would know where he was. He had caught a snatch from a news bulletin on the radio. It was reporting that two men had been located in the wreck of the rig, still alive. It named him. "Commander Frank Gaile, one of the Royal Navy's experts on submarine escape is in charge of operations. He is reported as being hopeful of getting both men out of their underwater prison before nightfall." I wonder who reported me as saying that. Journalist's licence, I suppose. The boys'll be loving it. They'll be watching that ruddy telly and seeing all the pictures those planes were taking this afternoon. They were quick on to it. Within an hour of reporting a contact in the hut, the planes were out like bees round a honey pot. Yes, the boys will be lapping it up and their mother will be praying that I'm not diving.

He pushed himself up off the sill and stretched. "I think I'll turn in for a bit, Captain, if that's all right with you."

"Sure thing. You go ahead. Take my bunk if that bastard Bright's not already in it."

"Thanks, but Strang found a spare cabin on the passenger deck. Have you got someone to spell you up here?"

"The bosun usually does but I'll leave him be. That was him wound round the windlass. He's probably still trying to get his breath."

"You can't spend the whole night up here."

"Why not? I've done it before. Anyway, I slept most of the afternoon. Don't worry, Commander. You go and get turned in."

"All right but call if you want a break. Strang or I could give you a spell. If you'd trust us with your ship, that is."

Johnny laughed. "If I was tired enough."

"Good night, then."

The other voice was unexpected. "I think I'll go down too."

"Who's that?" barked Ellam.

"It's that bastard Bright, Johnny," said Roger coming from the far side of the wheelhouse. "I've been here all the time."

"Well, bully for you, mate. I thought you'd be down below spewing your toe-nails up."

"No. I'm not a professional, of course. Not like you or the commander, Johnny, but I make out." He staggered and grabbed for a hold as the ship lurched into a big sea and tons of water hid the bows. "It's wonderful, isn't it. The power of it."

"Is that your trouble then?"

"How's that again?"

"Your trouble. You know, we all have some sort of trouble. Is that yours? Power mania."

Roger chuckled. "I hope not. It's a bad trouble."

"That's good. I was getting worried. You and me, Mr. Bright, we don't seem to get on so well. I was thinking maybe when you get back to that office in London you'll be getting rid of me."

"Why should I do that? I don't sack men for impertinence. Only for incompetence." He walked across to the starboard door. "By the way, Johnny, we must have a chat one day about how that mine wasn't sighted in time." He slid the door open and the howling gale added the exclamation point to his words.

The cabin was warm and bright. The lights and the curtained ports, the carpet and the gaily coloured furnishings seemed to insulate it from the storm outside. The noise filtered through, and the trembling of a wave thundering on board, but none of it seemed to be part of the cosy world inside. Roger looked at the bunk, then at the settee. He shrugged. Why disappoint the boy captain? The bunk it is. He flung off his coat and stepped out of his boots. He piled the pillows up at the forward end of the bunk and stretched himself on the soft mattress. He smiled as he thought of Johnny Ellam. He would be up there now, fuming at that last remark. But when the anger had burned away, the nagging doubt would remain.

Roger Bright made a point of broadcasting a little worry among his experts. He was fascinated by experts. He dealt with them all the time, he depended on them, he admired and liked them, he was appalled by their limitations but blessed them for having them for they gave him the carrot to dangle in front of their noses. Experts like Ellam, and Gaile, and Colney, and Tucker, each an authority in his own field, but all having to dance to Roger's tune. They were too exclusive, that was their trouble. Each knew his subject inside out but saw it in isolation. They could make a good case for a certain course. But ask them to relate it to other factors, criticisms from other experts, and all they could do was try to justify themselves. They knew they would have to accept compromise but they never did it gracefully. They were too expert. That was where Bright scored. Roger was an expert on nothing at all, but he had some expertise in almost every sphere where his work took him. Brad Tucker knew far more about drilling oil wells, but Roger knew a lot. Ted Colney could lose him on geology, but Roger was no fool about rocks. Even with things like ships and diving, he was quick to learn. If there was ever another time, ship captains and diving men would be in for a surprise. That was the trick; surprise the experts and you had them by the short hairs.

But all that apart, Roger Bright got a lot of pleasure from watching the experts in their chosen elements. It was a feeling of achievement, second-hand of course, even tinged with envy, but still achievement. Up on the bridge, watching Ellam jockeying his ship in these huge seas, apparently unafraid of anything nature could throw at him, seeing the dangers, finding the answer, seeing his answer fail, coming up with a new answer. Supremely confident and infecting those around him, dispelling fear. It was the same with Frank Gaile and his divers, Brad Tucker and his roughnecks. Although Bright felt this admiration he was never close to these men. There was a barrier between them; he used them, they were suspicious of him.

It was different with the roughnecks and roustabouts and truck drivers. They liked him. They had no axe to grind with him, nor he with them. He called them by name, he laughed at their jokes and told dirtier ones himself, he could take a drink, he wanted a day's work, but he was fair. For a boss, he was not a bad sort of bloke.

It was different with the Press. He got on famously with reporters. They were all fully paid-up members of the league of cynics.

It was different, and best of all, with the handful of men who thought as he did, who played the same sort of game for the same sort of stakes. Men like the Dutchman, van Sluys, and his own right-hand man in London, Harry Ashton. He had talked to Ashton that afternoon on the radio telephone. Communication between them was easy and complete. Each knew what the other would want to know. Each knew how much to tell because each knew the other's ability to turn a sketch into a completed picture.

They had joked about the slump in oil shares that would come on the Stock Exchange next morning. Inoco was not quoted in London so it was their competitors who would see millions knocked off the value of their stocks. The big boys would not worry; it would be a good time to buy. Ashton had told him a salvage ship was on its way from Hamburg. It would be at the wreck during Monday afternoon. They had talked of the problems of Offshore Five's destruction, the need for haste with the new rigs being built, the chances of leasing a rig from someone else, the arrangements for letting van Sluys know of Roger's decision about the Dutch options as soon as Colney could report. They had even talked of the fringe benefits of disaster; a more sympathetic hearing at the various Ministries, the free advertisement of the Inoco name in papers and on television, the irrational offers of help from competitors.

They had not talked of the immediate uncertainties. Could the Navy get Colney out alive and in time? The absolute deadline was 6 p.m. to-morrow, Monday. Did Colney have enough proof to warrant a go-ahead? They had not talked about these things because Harry Ashton could make no contribution. Roger was on the spot. He just had to wait and see, then make the decision.

He lay on the bunk, feeling the motion of the ship, listening to the wind and the slash and patter of spray on the bulkhead, trying not to think of what might happen to-morrow. Time enough to worry when it happened. Instead he thought about the bundle of Sunday newspapers the helicopter had dropped with the gas bottles. All the front pages were Offshore Five and Roger Bright in the thickest, blackest type. They had done him proud.

Chapter 13

The buzzing phone beside his head wakened Roger. He blinked up at the lights and shook his head. He peered at his watch. It was almost ten o'clock. He had been sleeping for nearly two hours. The phone buzz-buzzed impatiently. He wriggled up into a sitting position and answered it. It was Ellam and he sounded sour.

"Is that you, Mr. Bright, sir? This is your incompetent captain speaking. London wants you."

"I'll be right up." He heaved himself out of the bunk and steadied himself against the movement of the ship. It sounded wild outside. He stepped into his boots and fastened his coat. When he came out on deck the darkness blinded him for a few moments. Rain was lashing down, mingling with the spray and wrapping the ship in a drenching shroud. As his sight came back he could see curling wave tops streaking past at the level of his eyes, then the wave backs streaked with foam. The wind battered at his eardrums and snatched away his breath. The handrail he was gripping juddered with each impact as sea after sea broke over *Circe* and roared and swirled and gurgled overboard to make way for those following. Roger held tight to the rail. It was different this way. Now he was a little afraid. There was no expert there beside him.

He clenched his teeth and edged round the house towards the bridge ladder. He was in the full force of the gale now, his feet slipping on the wet deck, his face tortured by the lash of salt spray, his hands numb, his chest sore with the effort of breathing. He got to the ladder and clawed his way to the top. He crouched there in the lee of the dodgers trying to catch his breath. God's truth, people do this for a living. He ran for the door of the wheelhouse. Inside, he lay back against the closed door, gasping, grabbing for something to hold on to, trying to shake the noise and feel of the storm from his head. A red spot marked Ellam's position. His nose, his mouth, the line of his jaw were etched dimly as he puffed on his cigarette and it glowed brightly then faded.

"It's a bit damp out, isn't it. Sorry to haul you out."

"That's—that's all right." Bright felt his way uncertainly along the bridgefront. "Why the devil isn't there an inside stair up to here?"

"There is."

"What? Then why the hell am I scrambling round outside in that storm?"

"Well, Mr. Bright, sir, that's because of one of my silly rules. The inside stair's kept locked. It's only for the captain. Sounds daft, I know, but it helps to waken up the lads before they get here for their trick at the wheel."

Bright grunted. "Let me get to that R/T."

Johnny stepped round the pilot chair. "You know where it is. They're holding on. Reception's foul. You'd better use the headset." He stubbed out his cigarette and smiled.

Roger stumbled across the wheelhouse then reeled as a big sea struck *Circe* wide on the bow.

"Hold her up," barked Ellam. He stepped over close to the man at the wheel. "Watch her, will you, or we'll all be swimming."

"Sorry, Skipper."

Johnny went back to the windows and leaned on the sill. There was not much to see out there in the darkness but the grinning teeth of the waves and the lines of foam and, now and again, a flash of phosphorescence. The rest could be heard; rain, spray, wind, the boom of solid water on steel, the groaning of the ship in torment, but all muted by the closed wheelhouse. He could hear Bright talking to London.

"Speak up, Harry. The static's awful."

A pause.

"What was that? What about Paula?"

Another pause.

"Good God." Roger's voice was hushed, almost inaudible. "I said 'Good God'," he shouted.

There was a long interval as he listened to Ashton in London.

"Yes, Harry. Yes, of course. Of course I am. Just a bit of a shock. Yes, you do that. And take flowers. Roses, lots of roses. And Harry, give her my love."

Ellam watched in the dim light cast by the compass and the other instruments. He could see Bright standing quite still in front of the R/T, swaying with the motion of the ship. Then he slowly pulled off the headphones and hung them back in place.

"Anything wrong?" asked Johnny.

Roger looked round then came over and stood beside him, gripping the window ledge with both hands. "It's my wife."

"I'm sorry. What's the trouble?"

"She's—she's going to have a baby."

"Jesus Christ," roared Johnny. "I thought it was something serious. Urgent, they said. Very urgent. Get Mr. Bright. I thought it was something about the wreck. Then with you gasping about your wife, I thought she'd had an accident. And all the time it's just that she's in the family way."

"It's a bit of a shock. I didn't expect it."

"Who does? Family planning's all rot. Everyone I've ever met can't think how it could've happened."

"I suppose that's right." Roger's answers sounded automatic, like reflexes, as if his mind was numbed.

"Well, say something. Say you're pleased. Say you hope it's a boy. You are pleased, aren't you."

"Yes, yes, of course."

"That's better. Let me think. What've we got to wet

the baby's head?" Ellam went over to the rack on the after bulkhead and poured two mugs of coffee from a flask. He came back to where Roger was standing. "Come on, take it. Doctor Ellam's special brew for expectant fathers."

Bright took the hot mug and cradled it in both hands on the sill. He was hardly aware of the storm or of Johnny's voice. He was thinking about his wife. He was thinking about Paula in a way he had never done before. He was thinking of her as a mother. It was a new idea. It took a bit of getting used to. He knew all the other faces of Paula. Paula the Martini addict, Paula the gay divorcee, Paula the frenetic party goer and giver. That was not the whole story. There was Paula the bookworm, Paula the playgoer, Paula the sportswoman, Paula, one of society's most fashionable clothes horses. These were all the faces of Paula that appeared in the gossip columns. There she was always Paula Hartz, never Mrs. Roger Bright. "Wealthy American expatriate Paula Hartz. . . . Her husband is in oil." It was as if she kept him in an oil filled swimming pool like a pet seal.

But there was another Paula, the one Roger had fallen in love with, wooed, and won. The one he had seen at that party in New York, who had left the people she was with and come over and introduced herself. "I'm Paula. Tell me about yourself. All I know so far is that you haven't got a drink." Her voice was deep, almost gravelly, but it was like a voice he had been waiting for. He recognised it. There were other things he seemed to recognise. The way she stood, the way she held a drink or a cigarette, the way she laughed way down in her throat, head flung back, her whole body enjoying the joke, but with a trace of hysteria in it all. The way light shone on her hair, the way her lips opened when she smiled and the pleasure seemed to run up and show in her eyes. That was the Paula he had married despite all the warnings.

The warnings had come from all directions. Maybe that was why he ignored them. Roger liked to make up his own mind. They came in different ways; sidelong glances, whispered conversations stopping awkwardly as he approached, too hearty congratulations, one or two honest suggestions to think again. The bluntest warning came from her father.

Pop Hartz wanted to see his daughter married again. He liked Roger. He had never liked Paula's first choice and was glad to see that marriage ended. "Playboy, that's what he was, son. A playboy. Liked the good life, didn't have the money. Paula likes the good life, she's got plenty of money. Her grandmother's. We're pretty rich, son. That's the trouble. Never had to work for it. I work. I've always worked. I've made my money into a lot more money. You know about work. You'll make plenty. I like you, son. I'd like to see you and Paula married. But take a good long look at her first. She's full of good and bad. If it's going to work you're going to have to graft at making the good get rid of the bad. All right, so I can see you're not going to change your mind. That's fine. You've got my blessing. Here's a pointer, son. Paula's a woman. She needs a child. That's one thing she hasn't ever tried."

Well, she's going to try it now, Roger told himself. And from what Harry said she's as excited as hell. He went back over that call in his mind. She had phoned from Italy, asking for Roger. When she heard he was away, she spoke to Harry. He said she was so pleased with herself she hardly made sense. She had had tests. They were positive. She was flying home first thing in the morning. Harry was going out to the airport to meet her. He would take her to the flat. Harry's wife would look after her till Roger got back. They would take her roses, lots of them, from him. With any luck he would be there to-morrow night. Twenty-four hours, maybe less.

Maybe this would change everything. He hoped so. They had never talked about it. At first they had been wildly happy just being together. He had written off her father's advice. That was someone else who would be happy. Pop Hartz wanted grandchildren—that was something he could not buy. The trouble had started when Roger began work again. They took a plush flat in Mayfair; it was the kind of place Paula was accustomed to. It was too pricey for him so she paid. It did not seem to be important. Then she felt neglected. He worked too hard. Why work? There was plenty of money. She wanted to have fun. He tried to explain to her that his work was his fun. They were talking different languages. So he worked and she went to parties. She gave parties. They quarrelled, she threw things, then they would make up and go to bed and it would be all right till the morning. So much for the experts. If your sex life is well adjusted, you're at least half-way to a happy marriage. That's what they say. So what if your sex life's a wonder and the rest of the time you can't say a civil word to each other? Impossible, they say. The difficult we do immediately; the impossible takes just a little longer. It was an Inoco motto. But maybe this baby will change things. It started in bed and that's the place we understand each other.

Roger grasped the cold mug in his hands and smiled. I'm proud of myself. It's ridiculous. I've always thought it funny how men are so proud when they're going to be fathers, as if they had done something remarkable. It happens all the time. Every second of every day. Maybe several times every second, somewhere in the world. I'm more ordinary than I thought.

"Are you married, Johnny?"

"Not me. I've had a couple of near misses but both times I got a sudden yen to get back to sea."

Roger laughed. "So you haven't been through it. Hearing you're going to be a father, I mean."

"No. Who knows? Maybe someone tried to tell me. Thank God I was too far away to hear."

"It does something to you. It changes a lot of things."

"That I know. I've had mates who've been through it. It changes things all right. No more beer, no more football matches, cut down on the fags. Junior needs a walk in the park, Junior needs new shoes, Junior's Mummy likes to be kept company in the evenings. What about Junior's Daddy, that's what I say?"

"You'll come to it, Johnny."

"That's what I'm afraid of."

Roger watched a sea sliding over the bow, splintering, then gushing to and fro around the foredeck. "I'm off. Thanks for calling me. That was an important message." He walked round Ellam towards the door. "Oh, Johnny, I'm sorry I was a bit surly earlier on."

"That's all right. I deserved it. I needled you. I'll open that inside stair for you if you want."

"No, thanks. It's a good rule. The fresh air won't do me any harm."

Chapter 14

There was no storm down at the bottom of the sea to distract Ted Colney. Tucker had dropped into a fevered sleep. Occasionally he mumbled and struggled against the lashings Colney had fixed to hold him on the bunk when he was thrashing about in his delirium. Other than that there was only the sound of Colney's own breathing, faint gurgling sounds from outside as the sea moved against and round the hut, and now and again an eerie booming as a dangling piece of debris swung in the current and sounded against the main hull of the wreck.

There was no evidence of weather so bad that the rescue needed to be postponed. That thought kept coming into Colney's head. Had Tucker been right all along? Had the weather just been a story to excuse the abandoning of the rescue? No, that can't be. There's been no attempt to get us out yet. If they had run into snags they'd have told us. And there's Roger. He wouldn't give up without asking about that last core. He might have to leave us to die down here but not before he got enough to decide on these Dutch options. Did I tell him about that core? That's what Tucker was shouting when the air was shut off. No, Tucker was all confused, full of fever. I never said anything about the core or the theory. At least I don't think I did. Lord, I'm all mixed up too. I don't know what I did except that I capped these bolts and let them shut off the air. I hope I was right. Damn it, what am I thinking about. What difference does it make whether I capped the bolts or not. It doesn't matter what I do. If they can get us out of here, they will. If they can't, then we're both as good as dead and no amount of worrying will change that.

He told himself it was the darkness that was confusing him, that and not having Tucker to talk to or listen to, having had fresh air and now knowing it was being slowly used up again. That Navy man had said they would be back at daylight. What if the weather has not eased by then? It must, there's too much at stake. He smiled to himself. That's hardly a scientific attitude, Teddy. Things don't happen just because you want them enough. Not for you anyway. You wanted your marriage to succeed. It's a success, isn't it. Good-looking wife, two charming little girls, lovely detached house in a good London suburb, very good job. You've come a long way from that Pennine village, Teddy. Most people would give their eye teeth for what you've got. So what more do you want?

He shivered and pulled the blanket closer round him. He closed his eyes against the darkness. It was odd. He felt safer like that, less aware of his black prison. He let himself think about Carol and the children, Helen and Hilda. He let himself think about that ridiculous dog. It used to be good to think of them all in prospect or retrospect. It was when he was there that nothing seemed to be right. Maybe that was the trouble, too many women round him all the time when he was home. Even the dog was a bitch. No, that would be too simple. It all turned on aims, attitudes and values.

Carol and Ted Colney had got off to a wonderful start. He had had doubts; there was more than ten years' difference in their ages, he had spent all his adult life and most of his teenage years without any close relationship with a woman. But Carol had no doubts, she had enough confidence for both of them. She knew what she wanted and she was single minded enough to get it. She had got her degree. Now she wanted a husband and a home. She felt he needed her to look after him, to push him along in his career. She won the day. It was a good day, that first day, as were the few hundred to follow. They were together, she understood his work, they talked about it, they planned and he saw nothing sinister in these plans. He was in the grip of a revelation. Marriage was proving as exciting and stimulating an experience as any experiment, any theory. No longer the dreary round of landlady's menus. No longer the problems of laundry and mending. No longer the cold comfort of a companionless bed. Sex came to Ted Colney in his thirties with all the abandon of a teetotaller discovering alcohol. It was none the less satisfactory for his inexperience; that saved him from realising that Carol did not share his limitless enthusiasm.

Helen was soon on the way. Carol took pregnancy like a challenge. She was one of those women who never felt sick, whose skin, hair, even her eyes seemed to bloom with her condition. She would not be helped or treated like a semi-invalid. She read all the books and went to the pre-natal classes and did her relaxation exercises. She knitted and sewed, ordered a pram, cot, mattresses, practised bathing and cooking baby foods. She was the complete mother-to-be and she was already something less than the complete wife. But Ted did not notice this. He was too thrilled with the prospect of fatherhood. The baby came, Carol thought it looked like her own mother so she called it Helen. Ted thought it looked like a skinned rabbit but he was very proud. He boasted of her at the university laboratory and in the common room and piled wonder on to the surprise of his colleagues that this withdrawn, brilliant, but unconventional scientist should have been transformed into a doting husband and father.

Within four months Carol knew she was going to have another baby. She was quick to explain to her friends. "It's best to have them close together. It will be nice for Helen to have a playmate. An only child can be a terrible problem, don't you think." During this second pregnancy Carol, who now saw all her first line of objectives as being

within reach, raised her sights on to her cherished major
target, her husband and his career. From the beginning she
had dabbled in common-room politics. She collected gossip
and dispensed it. She ran coffee mornings and dainty tea
parties. She once tried a cocktail party which was a terrible
flop because Ted had not learned to drink at a rugby club,
did not know his way round the bottles, mixed all the drinks
wrongly, took too much himself and insulted two of the
professors. She took every opportunity to press her
husband's claim to a Senior Lectureship. Ted did not want
it. He was a researcher. He lectured only to pay the
bills. Soon after Hilda was born—Hilda was Carol's
grandmother's name—Carol accepted defeat. The lectureship had gone to someone else.

She was resilient. She had never wanted the post for her
Teddy. A psychiatrist might have seen significance in her
using that name for her husband. Teddy was far too
talented for the university. He should go into industry.
What industry needed talented geologists? Where are the
Sunday papers? They're always full of well-paid jobs.
Oil. Yes, of course. That was where Teddy should be. In
oil. That would be a real career. Money, prestige,
respectability, opportunity; in middle-class quantities but
more than that she never wanted.

Her campaign to redirect her husband from his chosen
career in the backwater of his redbrick university was not
subtle. She wanted to be away. Her weapon was per-
sistence. It came up at every meal. It even came up in bed,
dangled as a prize for which she would succumb. Her two
children were now to be her purpose in life. Ted Colney
was already launched on the steep slope to being a mere pro-
vider. He surrendered without much fight. At that time
he still felt that sacrifice was sometimes necessary if people
wanted to live together. And oil could be interesting,
especially with these new offshore techniques they were
trying out.

Inoco were glad to have him. His first tour was to be in

Venezuela. Carol decided to stay behind in England, because of the children of course. Venezuela was hot, the water and the sanitation would not be good, there were spiders, snakes, natives, and there always seemed to be a revolution going on. They bought a house in London. Carol had always wanted to stay in London. Ted was away for a year. He enjoyed his work but he had to live in bachelor quarters and he was miserable. He had none of the robust appetites of his colleagues. He missed his wife, his children, his home. He spent the whole year looking forward to that long leave, to tell Carol about his work, to tell her life could be good out there in South America, to play with his children. That leave was the beginning of the end of his illusions. The house was beautifully kept, the children were turned out like dolls, charming but already restrained by good manners which seemed foreign for toddlers. And when he made love to his wife, he felt he was despoiling an altar.

He did a two-year tour. He had some success with his work. He came home, hopefully, with the news that he was to go to the Persian Gulf as chief geologist on a new offshore exploration. Carol was very impressed. Of course the Persian Gulf would be even hotter and less sanitary, and Teddy would be away out on his oil rig all the time. No, she would stay at home. They had a new house, a detached one in a very good district. The girls were at kindergarten and there was a frightfully good private school for girls close by. The house needed a lot doing to it but Carol would enjoy that.

He did two years that time in the Gulf. The company made him take a break after a year. He went up into the mountains of Iran and came back refreshed to find a new man in charge of the offshore search—Roger Bright. Together they brought in two wells where Inoco's competitors had failed. Back to London. The house was transformed. It was like something out of a glossy magazine. He believed Carol when she said it was worth twice what they had paid for it and it had cost her less than half as much to do it. The girls were both at school, togged out in smart, restrained uniforms, bowing and curtsying and being so polite to their father that he felt he was living through some mad dream. The master bedroom was so feminine it would have excited a eunuch, except for the twin beds and the dressing-room where the master could hide his masculinity.

Ted Colney was an orderly man. He liked neatness but he liked comfort too. He began to loathe the plumping up of cushions when he rose from a chair, the stowing away of a magazine carelessly flung down on a table, the shouldering of a mackintosh draped on a banister rail, the baby talk scolding of the toy dog for lying on a settee. He began to loathe his house, his wife, his children. He began to loathe their senseless standards and attitudes, the coffee mornings, the charity teas, the kids' parties, everything. For the first time he thought of walking out. But he did not walk out. He went back early to another tour in the Gulf.

He thought a lot about leaving his wife. He even thought of dabbling in adultery to see if that brought him relief. It was easily available. But he never dabbled; adultery seemed far too complicated to be any sort of cure. His work was the nearest he got to finding an answer. His work gave him satisfaction and his call to join Roger's North Sea team excited him. This was something quite new. His wife was delighted with his news. The North Sea was so topical. Her friends would be very impressed. That was how his marriage was when he came out to join Offshore Five. That was how it still was unless Carol's message meant something.

Tucker was mumbling and struggling on the bunk. Colney stretched out and felt for the Texan's forehead. It was hot and damp. He wiped it dry with a handkerchief and, switching on the torch for a few seconds, forced some water between the moving lips.

The geologist lay back and rubbed at his arms to warm

them. Could that message be something more than the right kind of sentiment to express when your husband is trapped ninety feet under the sea? He shook his head. It's my fault. I've let it happen. I should've been tougher. I can be tough when I'm looking for oil. Maybe I should have been more understanding too. I wonder if it's too late to make a fresh start? The thought appalled him but his mind would not let go. "She sends her love. From the children too. She says to hurry and come home."

Dear God, get me out of this dark tomb, let me tell Roger Bright about the unique structures, and I promise I'll go back to that dreadful house and really try.

Chapter 15

Nine in the morning—Monday. The wind had died before dawn. Now it huffed and puffed in faint spasms from every point of the compass. The sky was covered with cloud but it was high and the light was good. It was the sea that was worrying the men on *Circe*'s bridge.

They had been there since daybreak; Bright, Gaile and Strang. Ellam had been there all night and was now sitting up in the pilot chair with his legs braced against the bridge-front to stop the chair swinging as the ship bucked and rolled. The sea had clung to the power bequeathed it by the gale. The steep, white-lipped, foam-backed waves had gone to be succeeded by an ugly, short, confused swell which heaved and swirled first one way then the other. It was a dangerous sea for diving.

Gaile lowered his binoculars. "What do you think, Captain?"

"I'm easy. I'll take her in if you want. But I'm only the skipper. You'd better ask Mr. Bright; he's the owner."

"What about it, Mr. Bright?"

"You're the experts. I want these men out of there as soon as possible."

"The ship shouldn't be in any danger. The problem's how safe it is to work below in this sea."

"That puts the decision back in your court, Commander."

Gaile nodded and stared out at the triangle of buoys marking the wreck. "We'll go in."

"Good," said Johnny, letting the chair swing and stepping

out of it. "I'm getting corns on my arse sitting around here doing damn all."

"Signalman." A rating answered Gaile's summons. "Tell *Blackamoor* we're going to moor and resume operations. Now, Captain, what about it?"

Ellam was searching the sea with the glasses. "That's a good question. I can't see that float we left to mark the hut. Your boys are going to have to feel around down there for it."

"How good a guess can you make at mooring right over it?"

"Do me a favour, Commander. I maybe wasn't at Dartmouth but I do know how to fix my ship's position. I've got a round of bearings on the wreck buoys. If they haven't dragged during the night, I'll do you a pretty fair guess."

"Good man. Rope and wire again?"

"No, the angle's wrong. That sea's all over the place but most of it's coming from the north-west, I was thinking of running right over the wreck, dropping one anchor on the far side where it won't foul anything, then backing her down into position. Then we can pick up that wire to steady her stern."

"That's good. If you don't get her plumb over the hut first time we can always run a rope out to that leg again and haul her into position with it."

Ellam nodded. "That'll give us a bridle for'ard and still leave us one anchor for that lifting job. Well, let's get started." He switched on the public address to call the crew to stations and the exhaust note hurried as he speeded the engines to drive *Circe* in over Offshore Five.

It was almost ten o'clock when Ellam announced he was satisfied. The workboat was in position, held by an anchor and a rope from the bow, and a wire from the stern to the kedge. The sea was losing its power as every minute passed but the little ship was still pitching and rolling uncomfortably. Gaile and Strang were down on deck with their men. As soon as Ellam gave the word two divers went over the side to find the geology hut and send up a marker. Six or seven minutes passed before the telephone confirmed that they had found the hut. Gaile let go his breath and watched for the plastic marker to break surface. It popped up off the starboard beam. The commander grinned and climbed the ladder to the bridge.

He shook his head and clucked his tongue at Ellam. "Bad show, Captain. You're at least twenty-five feet off the bulls-eye."

Johnny joined in the joke. "Twenty-five feet, you say. That is bad. Twenty-five feet, that's three hundred inches. That's bad shooting in a place as small as the North Sea."

They both laughed then talked about adjusting the moorings. It took ten minutes of heaving and slacking to get *Circe*'s after-deck plumb over the hut. By then the hoses were connected to the Cox's bolts, the loudspeaker was in position, the Sonar gear suspended, and the cutting equipment was being lowered. Gaile went back down on deck. He picked up the microphone and licked his lips. This was the first moment of truth that morning. They were back on site and ready to pluck these two men up from the bottom of the sea. It was less than sixteen hours since he had cut off their air supply. They would be a bit groggy but nothing more than that; the enriched air he had fed in last evening would have seen to that. But had anything else happened in the night. Had the huge pressure fractured the shell and let the water in? Had the darkness and the isolation and the fear of being deserted pushed their minds over the border of sanity? Remember that commotion in the hut last evening. He cleared his throat.

"Hallo there. Hallo there. Mr. Colney. Mr. Tucker. Do you read me? Do you read me? We are back in position now. We are back in position now. The air hoses are connected again. The hoses are connected again. Take the caps off the bolts. Uncap the bolts, please. We are ready to give you air. Tap three times when the caps are off the bolts." He kept calling, repeating the instructions. All the time he watched the Sonar operator. It seemed an age before the man looked up and nodded. He was getting some sort of reaction on his headphones. The commander stopped talking and waited. The man fiddled with the controls, nodding his head slowly, then he looked up and grinned. He held up three fingers.

"Thank God," said Gaile quietly. "Give them that air, Lieutenant." He turned away and made for the bridge. The stage was set. Now he had to think his plan over step by step. It would be too late to discover flaws when they had happened. Half an hour to refresh the air down there in the hut; an hour after that for the two men to recover enough to co-operate in the rescue; then one more hour and the poor devils would be up out of there. He checked his watch. Two and a half hours. Just after one o'clock. Nice time for lunch. Always assuming everything goes according to plan, of course. God, but I'll need luck. Luck with the final cutting to free one side of that deck, luck with getting these two men, one with a broken leg remember, into that escape chamber, luck with pressurising the chamber, luck with tipping the hut through ninety degrees to bring that outer door facing down. Then luck with getting the door open, luck with getting the diver in and the men out, one at a time; luck with the ascent and the problem of men holding on to breath which will kill them if they fail to get rid of it. Yes indeed, lots of luck.

Ellam and Bright were in the wheelhouse drinking coffee from white china mugs. Gaile told them the air supply was flowing again.

"Thank goodness," said Roger. "Are they all right down there? Have you talked to them?"

"They can't be too bad. They took the caps off the bolts to let the air in. I'm not bothering them for a bit till they get their lungs full of fresh air."

"Have some coffee," suggested Johnny, handing over a mug.

"Thanks."

"How long till you get them out?" asked Bright.

"It depends. Two or three hours if we're lucky."

Bright looked at his watch. "Good."

The commander drank some coffee and took the cigarette Johnny held out to him. "What's the deadline, Mr. Bright? I know you want to talk to this Mr. Colney. Is there some time limit?"

"I must talk to him this afternoon."

"That should be possible. But remember I can't guarantee anything. There's a hell of a lot of things can go wrong with this kind of operation."

"I know, Commander. You've done a great job already. I know you'll finish it."

"I hope so." He turned to Ellam. "Let's go into the chartroom and talk about this lifting job with the anchor."

Bright saw that the two wanted to be alone. "I'll just call London and let them know what's happening."

"You do that," said Johnny. "If you hurry you'll catch the afternoon editions."

There was a steely ring to Bright's laugh. "Someday, Johnny, someone won't realise you're always joking."

Gaile watched. He's a complicated character, that Bright. He's got as many facets as a well-cut diamond. There, just now, in that laugh was the measure of him. Hard, ruthless, smooth. Funny to think that's the same man who was boasting this morning about his baby-to-be. I could've sworn then he was proud just like any other new father.

Half an hour.

They had planned the use of the anchor as far as they could. They would have to play it off the cuff when it all started. Gaile went down on deck and called the hut on the loudspeaker. He told Colney to open the inner door, the one from the laboratory to the vestibule, if it was shut. He explained that if it had been shut, the air in there would be stale by now. He told Colney to be careful for that door opened inwards. If the vestibule had become open to the sea, the inner door would blast open as soon as the locking handles were released and that would be the end of any rescue. He told Colney to open the handles one at a time. He would soon see if there was any seepage from the other side. Gaile said not to worry if there was water in the vestibule. They could still go ahead by using the lab itself as an escape chamber. He checked the responses to his questions and instructions with the Sonar man. The inner door had been shut. There was no sign of leakage as the handles were swivelled off. The door was open. There was no water in the vestibule. Gaile lit a fresh cigarette and inhaled deeply. It's my lucky day.

An hour. Noon.

The doctor had talked to the hut, giving instructions that Tucker's legs should be strapped together before he was moved. The divers had fired a bolt into the vestibule. That bolt was now connected to its hose. Colney had been instructed not to uncap that bolt till he was told. Through that bolt and hose the chamber would be pressurised. The cutting of the deck supports was almost finished; soon the divers would be fixing the chain with which *Circe* would haul the hut on to its side. Commander Gaile was ready to tell Colney and Tucker exactly what they had to do.

"Hallo there. Hallo there. Commander Gaile here. Everything is going according to plan. I am now going to tell you what we are going to do and what we want you to do to help us. This will put you in the picture. After that I will give you instructions one at a time and ask for an acknowledgment when you have completed each task. If you are hearing me clearly, please tap five times."

The rating on the listening gear reported the tapping.

"Good. You are receiving me loud and clear. Here is the plan. We are going to use the space between the outer and inner doors of the hut as an escape chamber. You will be told to move into that space and close the inner door behind you. We will then tilt the deck on which the hut stands so that the outer door of the chamber faces downwards. In other words, the side of the chamber with the outer door in it will become the bottom of the chamber. You will then be told to unlock the handles on the outer door and uncap the bolt we have just placed in that chamber. Through that bolt we will pressurise the chamber to the same as the water pressure outside. The door will then fall open and the chamber will be open to the sea. The pressure will keep the water out. A diver will come into the chamber and instruct you how to escape. Just do exactly what he tells you and you will quickly be on the surface. He will guide you up and there will be a rope to hold on to. There is nothing to worry about, gentlemen. We will have you up in time for lunch. Give three taps if you have followed me this far."

The commander waited for the Sonar man to report.

"Good. Now, Mr. Colney, I will give you your first job. I want you to shift Mr. Tucker into that chamber between the inner and outer doors of the hut. Take your time. We realise it will not be easy. There is no hurry. Sit him up with his head at the opposite end of the chamber to where the bolt is. Acknowledge this instruction with two taps, then give six taps when you have finished the job."

The rating reported two taps and Gaile laid down the microphone. He lit a cigarette and went over and leaned on the rail. Now he just had to wait. There would be a lot of waiting in the next hour or so. He hated waiting. He wished he was down there diving. He looked out over the sea. It had lost most of its power. Only an occasional swell rocked *Circe*. He looked up at the sky. The cloud was lower and darker, rain laden, but there was no trace yet of new wind. *Blackamoor* was moored to the east and a cutter was chugging across towards the workboat. An aircraft was circling low over the site. More pictures for the thrill-hungry millions.

"How are things going, Commander?" It was Roger Bright.

"They're going. No snags so far. You'll just have to be patient, Mr. Bright."

"I know." He looked hard at the officer. "This rescue means a lot to you, doesn't it?"

"Two men's lives would mean a lot to anyone."

"No, I didn't mean that. I meant the actual rescue. Proving you were right, proving you can get men out from down there when most people would have given up long ago."

Gaile dropped his cigarette in the water. "I don't think I follow you. Excuse me, I've got work to do." He walked over to the men at the control post. Damn that bloody man. He sees through me like an open door. It's as if I'd told him how much I want success, how much I want all the naval boards to know they were wrong, to prove to them I'm of the calibre that deserves promotion. It's as if he knows I despise myself for thinking that way. Damn Roger Bright. Damn Frank Gaile too.

He listened to the reports from the divers. All the cutting was finished. The chain was in position waiting to be hooked on to *Circe*'s starboard anchor. The special light that Roger had brought out from Yarmouth that first night was ready for lighting up that door. That had been Strang's idea. A good one. It would give the two prisoners confidence to see light when the chamber was opened to the sea. He told the divers to wait. He wanted to take the microphone and ask Colney why he was taking so long to move Tucker into the chamber. But he held on to his impatience. He reminded himself that they had been down there in the darkness and the cold, probably without food, for more than a day and a half. One of them had a broken leg. No one could be sure what it might have done to their minds and their bodies. He waited.

At last the six taps were reported. Now for the most difficult bit of all.

"Hallo there, Mr. Colney. Good man. Now please stand by the two air bolts in the laboratory. That's the two bolts we first placed. Do not cap them till I tell you. Then cap them, go into the chamber with Tucker and close the inside door behind you. Tap three times when you are standing by the bolts."

Three reported.

"Thank you, Mr. Colney. We are now fixing lifting gear for tilting the hut. You may feel a few bumps. Do not worry."

Ellam was there beside him. "D'you want that anchor now?"

"Yes. Remember what we agreed. Lower it to sixty feet. Then we'll adjust the moorings to bring the anchor plumb over the hut. The divers'll guide it down from there till they fix the chains. Then we'll heave *Circe* back into position to give us the angle to tilt the hut."

"Roger, Commander. Or as we say in Inoco—Mr. Bright, sir."

Gaile laughed. "Remind me to buy you a drink when it's all over, Captain."

"I will too."

Gaile checked with the divers. They were ready below. One was up at the bow waiting to trace the anchor down. "Lower away," he bawled through the loud-hailer. At once he heard the clanking of the chain on the windlass, then Ellam's voice telling the bosun to stop before he had one shackle on deck. At the control post everyone was busy. The Sonar man and the telephone men connected to each of the divers were listening intently. Tape recorders whirred. A signalman was giving *Blackamoor* a running commentary on a walkie-talkie. The petty officer on the rack of air bottles was checking gauges. Lieutenant Strang was standing off in the rubber Gemini boat with one diver. Lookouts had already been posted bow and stern and in each wing of the bridge. A cutter from the frigate was there waiting to pick out the men as they came up and rush them across the gap to the warship in case they needed re-compression. There was still a lot of waiting to be done but everyone was ready for the rescue when it came.

One peal on the anchor bell and the windlass stopped.

Gaile pointed at one of the telephone men. He spoke to his diver telling him to come up the shot rope to sixty feet to rendezvous with the man tracking the anchor. The commander signalled up to Ellam on the bridge to start dropping *Circe* back on her moorings. There was a flurry of orders fore and aft, winches and windlass whined and clattered, and the float on the shot rope moved towards the bow as the workboat dropped back to plumb her anchor over the hut.

In position.

Gaile held up his hand and the noise and movement stopped. Now pray for no mistakes or that anchor will plunge down and crack that hut open like a rotten walnut. Lower away again. The windlass clanked slowly and the anchor sank down towards the hut. Stop. That's far enough. The divers are fixing the chains. *Circe* bucked in a sudden swell and swear words crackled on the phones as the anchor jerked in sympathy, scattering the divers. All right, no damage done, get on with it. Chains fixed. Heave away easy to take up the slack. Easy, easy. That's it. Hold on like that.

The commander started a new round of checks and instructions. Divers to check the chains under the hut deck. Stand by fore and aft to adjust the moorings. Lookouts, Gemini boat, air bottles.

"Hallo there, Mr. Colney. We are shutting off the air in the laboratory now. When it stops, cap both these bolts. Acknowledge this message with three taps, then give five when the caps are on."

Sonar reports three taps. Gaile signed to the man on the air bottles. The valves were swung shut. Sonar reports five.

"Thank you, Mr. Colney. Now go into the escape

chamber beside Mr. Tucker. Close the inner door and swing all the handles tight shut. Tap four times when you are in and the door is tight."

The two minutes till the tapping was heard seemed like a lifetime.

"Thank you. We are now going to tilt the hut. Be ready for the movement. Remember that the tilting will bring the outer door facing downwards. You will then be sitting with your legs across the inside of that door. Do not touch the door handles or the cap of the bolt till you are told. Here we go."

He laid down the microphone and wiped his sleeve across his face. He passed a message to the divers to tend the hoses, particularly the one to the escape chamber to stop it getting fouled by the anchor chain. He signalled Ellam to haul *Circe* back into position. Gaile heard the orders being passed and the windlass working and the reports being relayed from the divers but he was watching that float, willing it to come aft and abeam. It took minutes and they were like hours. At last. Now for the real moment of truth. The commander wiped the cold sweat from his face and licked his lips.

"Heave easy, Captain."

Gaile went to the rail and watched the ship's bow as the windlass took the strain. The first few links came in easily then the sound slowed as the weight came on the anchor chain leading aft under *Circe* at the angle calculated to give the right degree of tilt to the severed deck on which the geology hut stood. The windlass strained as more power was fed into it. A link clanked on the gypsy, then another, then only the complaining whine of the motor. The bow dipped under the weight and the commander saw the chain of the mooring anchor and the doubled rope to the leg of the wreck stretched taut across the water. They looked sure to give way. The windlass droned then clanked suddenly as a link came over the gypsy. Then another. Gaile let go of his breath and stepped back to the control post. The divers

169

were reporting movement. The deck was being prised up as planned.

That windlass is running too fast. "Easy," roared the commander. The sound slowed. "Vast heaving." The windlass stopped. Message to divers to check angle of hut.

Reply from No. 4. "I've got that light on. It's bloody marvellous. It's like Blackpool down here. All right, all right, what's the hurry. You need a bit more yet."

"Very easy," ordered Gaile. "A link at a time if you can."

One—two—three—four.

"That's it," from the depths.

The commander's raised hand signalled Ellam and the windlass stopped.

"Bang on," from No. 4. "The hose is clear."

Gaile listened to the reports as they came in on the phones. No loose debris in the way. Chains holding fast under the hut deck. Loudspeaker shifted round to the chamber side. He picked up the microphone. "Hallo there. Hallo there. Hope that was not too rough a ride for you. Are you ready to start again now? Four taps, please."

Four reported.

"Good. Uncap that bolt now, Mr. Colney. Five taps when it is off."

He checked his watch. The long wait was only forty-five seconds.

"Good man. Now sit down beside Mr. Tucker and kick off all the locking handles on the door under your legs. Don't worry. The door will stay shut. You may get a little seepage. Don't worry. Three taps when all the handles are off."

It was a minute and a half before the acknowledgment came.

"Grand. We are now going to pressurise that chamber. You will feel it in your ears. Keep swallowing or pinching your nose and blowing down it. Just breathe normally. When the pressure builds up that door will fall open. Stay

where you are. Do you hear me? Stay where you are
when that door opens. A diver will come in and instruct
you. Please acknowledge with four taps."

Four reported at once.

Gaile checked everything once more. The Gemini was
there, its big outboard revving. *Blackamoor*'s cutter had
moved up and had the end of the ascent rope on board.
The divers were all ready. No. 4 was going to do the
ascents, Tucker first, then Colney. The other divers were
standing by for emergencies. The lookouts were alerted.

"Blow her up." The petty officer swung the valves on
his bottles and the armoured hose jumped as the com-
pressed air flooded into it. The commander checked his
watch. Half a minute. Forty-five seconds. A minute.

"That's it, sir."

At the same time the No. 4 phone reported. "Door's
open, sir. Says it's a lovely sight, sir."

"Tell him to get on with it." God, we've been lucky.
Not a hitch. Gaile wiped at his face. Five minutes should
do it.

"The light's gone out, sir."

"Damn the light. He never had one before. Tell him
to get in there." He reached out to grab the phone.

"He's going in, sir."

"About time too,"

Another report from the diver. "No. 4's lines are tangled,
sir."

Gaile gritted his teeth. Too good to be true. I knew it.
I'll send one of the others in. No, give him time. He's
the best man. He'll soon clear himself. "Tell him to be
careful. It costs the Navy a lot to train divers." God's
truth! I'd better tell these two down there that there's
been a hitch. He picked up the microphone.

The call from the lookout on the bridge was loud and
clear. It made the hair on the commander's neck stiffen.
"Red one twenty. Man in the water."

Gaile grabbed the loud-hailer. "Strang. Man in the

water. Red one twenty." He shouted at the control crew. "Tell them to hold everything." Then he felt the microphone in his hand. "Don't move down there. Don't move."

The Gemini was already on its way round to hook the body and pull it inboard.

The commander stood at the side gripping the rail. He could feel the question all around him so he said it himself, in a whisper. "I wonder which of the poor bastards couldn't wait?"

Chapter 16

Colney and Tucker were both still down in the chamber.
They were confused and apprehensive. They had expected
a quick rescue after the door had fallen open and they had
seen the water, held back by the magic of the pressure but
not at all frightening lit up as it was by the floodlight
outside. They had had to screw their eyes up against the
light but they had not complained. That light had meant
the end of their ordeal of darkness and entombment. Then
the light was snuffed out and the order not to move barked
and boomed at them from the loudspeaker. They could
sense the emergency. They waited, knowing nothing of
the mangled body being fished from the sea and rushed
back to *Circe* for identification; the body of one of Offshore
Five's drilling crew trapped as the hut deck collapsed on top
of him, and freed to float up to the surface when the deck
was tilted. They waited, not knowing why the light
had suddenly gone out, not knowing that the diver was
tangled in the wreckage and was still trying to free himself.

"What the hell's keeping them?" growled Tucker.

"They'll tell us soon enough. Some little hitch. They'll
want everything to be exactly right before they take us out."

"If they take us out."

"They've got us this far. I don't suppose they did all that
work just for fun. Don't worry, Tucker. They'll get us
out all right."

Colney hoped his own fears did not sound in his voice.
Tucker needed encouragement. He was a different man
now his fever had left him. It was as if it had burned away

all his strength and his courage. From the time he came to in the morning it was clear that he no longer believed they would escape. He had asked the time. It was almost eight o'clock. That was a measure of the change in him. No shouting or cursing. Everything said quietly, almost inaudibly, in that tired croaking voice. He had not needed to remind Colney of the commander's promise to return at daylight.

Ted had tried to look at the Texan's leg, maybe clean away any pus that had collected. Brad told him to leave it be. What did it matter? They would choke to death before the leg killed him. The geologist tried desperately to drag Tucker back from his acceptance of inevitable death. He remembered incidents Brad had talked of in his demented monologue the day before. He spoke about them, asked about the people, the places. Brad said they were all history. He refused to talk or think about them. He was going to die. That was sure so he did not want to be reminded of what he was losing. Colney even talked about his own wife. He had never talked to anyone else about her. He told Brad how his marriage had not worked out, how he was now sure it could be saved, how he planned to go about it when he got back up into the world. Tucker told him he was kidding himself, about getting back to the surface and about making everything come right again.

Even when the sounds of the ship and the rattling anchor and the divers outside came through to them, the Texan was unconvinced. All right, so they were going to try again. They were going to pump in fresh air and keep them alive for a bit longer. Till the next bit of dirty weather. Till they were finished experimenting and had to admit they could not get the two men out. The new air brought a new problem. Tucker had not been able to smell in the fouled air of the hut. Now he got his smell back and he was quick to trace the stench to his own leg. What was the point of getting out now? Better stay and die than have to stomp around on a peg leg for the rest of his life. One-legged Tucker; that would be a great joke in the oil fields and the brothels.

He had not the strength to resist when Colney started dragging him towards the vestibule. He swore a bit as the little man dragged him on the mattress across the deck. Tucker was weak but he was still heavy. It took Ted a long time to skid his patient the few feet to the inner door. It took him longer to drag Tucker through the door into the vestibule. They were both exhausted when it was done. But Colney could not afford exhaustion. The booming voice was issuing more instructions. He crawled out and stood by the bolts in the laboratory. He felt the hut moving as the weight came on the chains. The voice sounded. He capped the bolts and scrambled for the door to the chamber. In. Swing the door shut. The sound was dull, metallic, final. Swing the handles shut. Twist them all tight. How many taps did the voice say? Three, four? Why is it always a different number? Four, that was it. He hammered four times.

Then came that tilting and with it the memory of the disaster. The sounds were the same, tearing metal, clanging, screeching, and from through in his lab the crash of instruments and bottles and beakers and books. His books, his note-books; he had left them in there. No use now, can't go back; it's all in my head, not to worry. The tilt was already steep. He grabbed at Tucker and held on to him. They were all mixed up together when the tilting stopped. Colney still had the torch strapped round his waist. It gave only a glimmer but it was enough for him to see that the outer door was now underneath them. He dragged at the Texan till he was sitting up with his back against the bulkhead, his strapped and splinted legs stretched out across the door, his feet resting on the steel beyond the door.

Uncap the bolt. There was little room to move about. He squeezed over to the other end of the chamber and unscrewed the cap. Back beside Tucker and struggling to kick all the handles off. He used the torch again for a few seconds to check that none had been missed. Three taps on the steel beside him. Then the voice, the swoosh of high-pressure air, the stabbing pain in his ears. And suddenly that glorious blaze of light and the water lapping at the backs of their legs but unable to harm them.

"Jesus," breathed Tucker. "It's going to work."

His new hope was short-lived. The light went out and the voice left a new and agonising question mark in their minds. The wait in the darkness, with the now menacing sound and feel of water around them and touching them, seemed interminable. It was barely three minutes.

"Hallo there. Hallo there. Sorry about all that, gentlemen. We had a spot of bother but it's all over. A diver will be coming in any second now. Good luck."

"They're so bloody polite with it all," said Tucker. "You'd think we was having tea with a duchess."

Colney had no time to reply. He felt his legs being pushed aside and heard water swirling and splashing. He switched on the torch and in the pale glow saw the grotesque shape of the diver's head sticking up out of the sea. A hand appeared and pulled aside the face mask.

"Move over, mateys, I want to come in."

Colney pulled his legs up into his chest and the diver was suddenly sitting opposite him, his legs still dangling down through the open doorway.

"That's better. Sorry about the hold up, mateys. I got myself all tangled up outside. Now which of you's Mr. Tucker? That'll be you. They said you had a gammy leg. Right, now listen. You'll go up one at a time. It's as easy as shelling peas. I'll go up with you. Outside there's a rope. It's got a knot every three feet. Get your hands on that rope and your troubles are over. Take a deep breath before you drop into the water. Remember you've got the same as four lungfuls of air inside you. By the time you get to the top you've got to get rid of the lot. Every thirty-three feet, that's eleven knots, you've got to blow out. That's important. But don't worry. I'll be with you. If you don't blow, I'll punch it out of you. No offence, of course. It's all in a good cause. Have you got all that? Good, now let's get you ready. Put this thing on. Over your head, that's it. Now tie the tapes behind you. That's it, your mate's doing it for you. You're Mr. Colney, is that right. Good, here's one for you too. Put it on so you're ready. Now here's the drill. That's a float collar. There's a canister on the front. That's it. Now that will blow the collar up when you pull that cord. This is for the surface, just in case we miss the recovery boat. Don't pull the cord till you hit the surface. Then pull it, or I'll pull it for you, the collar'll blow up and it'll keep your head out of the water till you're picked up. Got that? Good. Now don't worry, Mr. Tucker. I'll be with you all the time. I'm giving you the drill just in case you lose me. But you won't. Now, quickly, tell me what happens."

Tucker went slowly through the drill.

"Top of the class. Now let's get you sitting up on the edge of the hatch here with your legs in the water."

Tucker could not move in the small space with his pinioned legs.

"Wait," said Colney. "Bend down, try and put your head between your knees. That's it. Now I'll lift his body," he said to the diver, "and you swing his legs over and down into the water."

"You're a smart lad, matey. You don't need me to help you."

Brad bent forward and Colney struggled to his knees. He grasped the Texan under the arms and prised him up off the deck. The diver swung the splinted legs across and got them into the water at one corner of the doorway. Ted lowered the big man slowly till he was sitting on the edge of the deck with his legs hanging down into the water.

"It's lovely and cold," said Tucker.

The diver slipped back into the water. "Remember now. A deep breath. I'm ready when you are." He clipped his face mask back in place and ducked out of sight.

Brad sat there on the edge of the doorway. "Now I really believe it, Colney. Thanks, pal. I'd never have got this far without you. You're all right, Limey. I'll buy you a beer when you come up."

"I don't drink beer but thanks all the same."

"All right, so I'll buy you what you do drink. That bastard's pulling on my leg. Here goes." He took a big breath and dropped into the water.

The water splashed up then the quiet and the dark settled on the chamber. The torch was quite dead now. Colney felt his way across the deck and slipped his legs down into the water. Tucker had been right. It was cold but somehow refreshing.

I wonder how long it will be. I never asked. Not long, I suppose. A few minutes. Then I'll be up on the surface. Roger will be there. He'll want to know about the core and the unique structures. He'll be thrilled. He'll be glad he listened to me. And when it all comes out, those other geologists will look pretty sick. First rule of science. Never assume. Never accept other people's ideas unless they are proved. They forgot that rule. They'll have to eat humble pie at my table. They'll be falling over themselves to show that they never excluded the possibility of such a freak formation. Then I can tell them it's not a freak. Then I can tell them there are lots of unique structures still to be found. And they'll have to listen to me. And they won't know where to look.

Lord, where's that diver? It's ages since he went up. I'll just have to wait. It's funny, the darkness is much worse without Tucker. He seemed quite friendly at the end. Fancy that. I'd never have believed I could get friendly with him.

What's that? Someone pulling at my leg. No, no it's that door swinging about in the water. I can feel the handles with my feet.

Carol will be surprised when I come home and really start trying to be a husband. She won't like it at first maybe, having things changed after all these years. But she'll come round. She'll see it my way. She'll see it's the best way. The children too. It'll be a shock for them to have a real father. It'll do them good.

Where is that damned diver? My legs are getting cold. He's been an age. He said he'd be back. He did say that, didn't he.

The hut lurched as a swell caught *Circe*.

What's happening? What did that diver say? He gave me the float collar and said to put it on so I'd be ready. That's right. Then he said not to move. No, that was the voice, the time before. The diver said I didn't need any help from him. That's right. That's what he said. Lord, I'm a fool. I've been sitting here waiting and he's not coming back. They're waiting for me up there on the surface. What was the drill again? Yes, I remember. Take a deep breath. Drop into the water. Get a hold of the rope outside. There's a knot every three feet. Eleven knots and blow out. That's thirty-three feet. That makes sense. Sea pressure increases one atmosphere every thirty-three feet. I'm at four atmospheres so I've got the equivalent of four lungfuls of air at surface pressure. That's it, of course. So I've got to get rid of that extra air as the pressure decreases. It's simple. Then when I break surface, I pull the cord on this collar and I'll float till they pick me up. What a fool I've been. Deep breath now.

He pushed himself off the edge of the doorway and splashed down into the dark cold water.

Chapter 17

The diver's report came in first.

Gaile was still watching the cutter where Tucker was lying on a stretcher with the doctor bent over him. The commander already knew it had been a copy-book ascent. He had had the glasses trained on the top of the ascent rope when the man and the diver broke surface. The American's face had shown surprise, then his eyes shut tight against the daylight, then his mouth relaxed as he took in the fact that he was up on the surface and safe.

"No. 4 says chamber's empty, sir. The second man's disappeared."

For a second, Gaile failed to take it in. Then the lookout's excited shout drove it home. "Green four five. Man in the water. Green four five. Man in the water."

As the commander grabbed for the loud-hailer he heard the roar of the Gemini's outboard. Strang had heard the lookout and was wasting no time. Gaile swung his eyes round to the starboard bow. There he was, the orange float collar holding his head up out of the water. There was no sign of movement. The bloody fool. The bloody fool. That was all Gaile could think. The bloody fool. I told him to wait.

The Gemini was there, Strang leaning out and dragging Colney on board. The commander was rapid-firing orders.

Through the loud-hailer. "Strang, the cutter. Pick up the doc."

To the cutter. "Doc, go with them. I'll warn *Blacka-moor*."

To the signalman on the frigate's walkie-talkie. "Tell *Blackamoor* to stand by for recompression."

The rescue boat was roaring back towards the cutter. Strang was holding Colney up with one arm and slapping his face with all his strength with his free hand. That's it, Lieutenant. You know what you're doing. Wake him up. Don't let him slip away. Slap him, punch him, shake him. Get his eyes open. Get him talking.

The Gemini surged alongside the cutter, slowed momentarily, the doctor tumbled on board and the craft accelerated away, slopping water over the low gunwale as the men sorted themselves out.

"*Blackamoor*'s standing by for recompression, sir."

Gaile nodded. Let's hope it's in time. Let's hope that's what's needed. The bloody fool. Why did he do it?

"What went wrong, Commander?" It was Roger Bright.

"He decided to come up on his own. That's what went wrong."

"Is he . . . dead?"

"Don't know. They'll do all they can for him. They've got all the gear there on the frigate."

Bright nodded slowly. His mouth was set in a hard line and his face was pale.

"They'll let us know, Mr. Bright. I know how important it is to you. To me too. Most of all it's important to Colney. Don't let's assume he's dead till we hear. Air embolism's pretty nasty but it doesn't have to be fatal, not if they catch it in time."

"Is that what's wrong with him?"

"Most likely. Embolism, it means bubble. That's why they were slapping and shaking him in the boat. Trying to stop that air bubble lodging in his brain."

"I don't follow you, Commander. How did this air bubble get there?"

"Wait a minute. I'll explain it to you." He went over to the control post and gave orders for the divers to start disconnecting the hoses. He shouted up to Ellam on the bridge. "About ten or fifteen minutes, Captain, then we can unhook that anchor from the hut."

Johnny asked about Tucker.

"He seems all right. I'm not sure about the other one yet." He came back to where Bright was standing at the rail. The cutter was chugging across towards the frigate to deliver the Texan. "Where was I?"

"You were going to explain about embolism."

"Yes. Well, it's like this. Colney was at a pressure of almost four atmospheres. That means the air in his lungs was about four times more than it would be at the surface. Same volume of course, compressed. As he came up he should have got rid of all that extra air. He probably didn't. The air expanded with the reduction of pressure and it had to go somewhere. It couldn't get out of his mouth so it forced its way through the walls of his lungs. Some may have stayed in his chest cavity. Some may have got into his bloodstream. If it has, he's got an air embolism."

"You said it's not always fatal."

"If it's left, it will be. Most often it sticks in the brain. That's why there's never much time."

"You mean that even if he recovers, the brain may be damaged?"

"Yes, but it's recovery that's important. After all, most of us only use about ten per cent of our brains most of the time.

"I don't think that's very funny, Commander."

"It's not supposed to be. It's a fact."

"Message from *Blackamoor*, sir." Everyone within earshot turned towards the signalman. "Recompression successful. No disability apparent."

There was a ragged cheer and everyone started talking. "Stow the chatter," roared Gaile. "You've all got jobs to do. Get on with them."

"Does that mean he's going to be all right?" asked Roger.

"It means he's already all right, thank God. That's the odd thing about embolism. You fling a man into a re-compression tank. He can't speak, his eyes are rolling all over the place, he can't understand what you say; he looks as if he's just about had it. You slam on four, five, maybe six atmospheres. Wham. And suddenly he's sitting there asking you what happened. The bubble gets com-pressed, starts moving again, and begins to dissipate. It's a weird and wonderful thing to see, Mr. Bright."

"I'm sure it is. It's fantastic." Roger's face had an eager look. "So I can see Colney, soon."

"No, not soon. He has to stay in the tank for a bit. It takes a little time to bring him back to normal pressure."

"How long?"

"I'd need to look up the tables for that. But offhand I'd say thirty-six, maybe forty-eight hours, something like that."

"What?" barked Bright. "I can't wait that long. I've got to see him this afternoon."

"You can't. Even for you, Mr. Bright, some things are impossible."

"There must be a way, Commander. This is more important than you can imagine. I must speak with Colney this afternoon."

"You can speak to him. That's no problem. Just go over to *Blackamoor* and pick up the phone on the outside of the tank. The doc's in there with him. They need a phone to talk to the crew on the controls."

"Why didn't you say that in the first place?"

"You didn't ask, Mr. Bright. You said you wanted to see him. There aren't any windows in the tank."

"I see." Roger's voice was chilly. "Could you arrange to put me on board the frigate?"

"Of course." Gaile stepped over to the signalman. "Ask *Blackamoor* to send a . . . no, to send back the Gemini boat at once." He smiled. Yes, the Gemini boat's just the thing for Mr. Roger Bright. It's fast, low, and likely to ship a lot of water. Maybe a soaking will remind him that it's usual to say thank you when people have done you a favour, even if it is only their job. "It should only be a few minutes, Mr. Bright. I hope you find out all you want." He turned away up the ladder to the bridge. As he got to the top he felt a puff of wind on his face and heard the sizzle of rain on the sea. He looked up at the black clouds with the long streamers heralding new wind. You've been cheated. We've got them out.

Roger waited at the rail. He could see the rescue boat speeding across the gap towards *Circe*. He felt the rain on his neck and turned his collar up against it. Rain, wind, sea; nothing mattered now. He was going to talk to Ted Colney. He was going to find out about that last core, whether or not it confirmed Colney's ideas about unique structures. He was going to be in time to decide on these Dutch options. He checked his watch. Just gone two o'clock. Plenty of time.

The Gemini came alongside and a sailor handed him down into it. Strang got out and left him alone with the coxswain. The boat went away fast towards the frigate. An occasional wavelet slopped on board but it was as nothing with the rain now slanting down in a solid curtain. Bright huddled down, ignoring his drenched clothes, his eyes fixed on the frigate. An officer met him as he stepped on board. Tucker was in good shape. He was demanding whisky, steak and cigars. They thought they could save his leg. Colney was apparently none the worse for his unexpected free ascent. Bright was led along to the after deck where the recompression tank sat under a weather screen of awnings. It looked like an out of place bank vault, with the huge locking wheel on the door. The officer unhooked the phone and handed it to Roger, then whirled the handle of the call bell. The doctor spoke first then put Colney on.

"Hallo, Ted. Roger Bright here. How are you?"

"I'm fine, Roger. I've got to stay in here for a couple of days, they say."

"That's right. And you do what they say. You're valuable property. You scared the wits out of us when you popped up out of the sea like that."

"Sorry about that. I must have got mixed up with the orders. The diver was away such a long time, then I thought he had meant me to go up on my own. He had told me all about how to do it. It seemed easy. So I started up. He said there was a knotted rope but I couldn't find it. I blew out just like he said. Then I found some sort of chain. An anchor chain, I suppose. I started coming up it. I must have forgotten to blow out. My chest got sore. Then my head felt funny. I blew out some more then but it was difficult. I knew I had to blow out but, somehow, I couldn't always do it. Then I got this sore chest and head again and I thought I could see light above me, so I pulled the cord on that collar thing. I must have passed out then."

"You certainly did but not to worry. All's well and all that."

"How's Tucker? They say he made it. They say they can save his leg."

"Yes, Tucker's fine. He's apparently playing hell down in the sick-bay. He's demanding whisky and cigars."

"Cigars? Are you sure he asked for cigars."

"So they tell me. What's the matter? Why shouldn't he want a cigar?"

"No, no reason, I suppose. I'm—I'm surprised, that's all. He told me down in the hut that I'd cured him of smoking."

"I'll bet he did, Ted. Down there, it must have been easy to make good resolutions. It's different when you're back up in the real world. What good resolutions did you make?"

"None," Colney replied quickly. "None, except to tell you about my unique structures."

"Good man. Don't break that resolution. I'm waiting.

There's still time to confirm those Dutch options. How was that last core?"

"It was good, Roger. Just what I expected. A few hundred more feet and we'd have struck."

"Great. So there was some sort of show of oil in that core."

"No, nothing at all. But that's what I expected. That salt's completely impermeable. I've got all the proof I need. The unique structures are there. My theory's right, Roger. It's a real breakthrough."

"Ted, this is fantastic news. But tell me about this theory of unique structures. I've got a decision to make. I trust you, of course. But now I have to have an idea of what it is we're going after."

"I understand, Roger. I'll tell you."

He did tell Bright. He told him about the Zechstein Sea and the creasing and folding of the salt crust. He told him about the domes and how they had grown hollow caverns inside themselves, he told him of how the reservoir rocks had spilled their oil into the hollow domes and been sealed off by the salt. Roger squatted outside with the phone to his ear, the rain beating a tattoo on the canvas over his head, and his eyes opened wide and he licked at his lips, suddenly dry.

"That's it, Roger. Briefly, of course, but that should be enough for you for now."

Bright cleared his throat. "Ted, it's astounding if it's true."

"What d'you mean, 'if it's true'? It is true."

"Yes, but what you're saying is that there are great caves of liquid oil sealed off down there. That is what you're saying, isn't it."

"Yes."

"But nobody believes that's possible. I'm not a geologist but I always thought that lakes of oil, pools of oil, were just what the ignorant public thought about oil fields."

"So it was. And geologists were so sure they were

right that if they ever came across evidence that suggested liquid deposits, they ignored it, explained it away as a seismic error, anything as long as it wasn't oil. Now we know better, Roger."

"Reserves? Does that first estimate of ten times the breakeven figure hold good?"

"Fifty times, Roger. At least fifty times."

Bright's breath whistled through his teeth. "That really will be a strike."

"I told you, didn't I. I told you months ago that Offshore Five would be a good investment."

"You did that, Ted. And you were right. You've really given me something to think about."

"Don't just think about it, Roger. Get these leases. You do believe my theory, don't you."

"Stop worrying, Ted. You know me. Am I the kind of man to turn my back on a goldmine like that? Am I?"

"No, no, you're not."

"Good, then that's settled. I'm proud of you, Ted Colney. Now I must get on to London and start making you famous. The Colney Theory of Unique Structures. It sounds good too."

"Thanks, Roger. I knew you would be with me."

"Can I phone your wife, give her your love?"

There was a long pause. "Yes, do that, will you. Phone her, phone her and tell her when they let me out of here I'll be home—as usual."

"Home as usual. It's as good as done. Take it easy in there, Ted. Don't do anything I wouldn't do. 'Bye."

He hooked up the phone and sat quite still. The whole thing stunned him with its scale and originality. It transgressed all the known facts about oil. But Colney had been right before. Bright's reputation rested to some extent on his support for Colney in the past when other experts were sceptical. Backing the well-fancied outsider was Roger's pet formula. If the risks were well calculated and the bet hedged, the returns could be enormous. This was not a bet he could hedge. The equipment available and the terms of the leases barred that. This time it had to be a straight choice between the favourite and the outsider. Bright had already convinced himself that the outsider would have his money.

All the way back in the boat he was oblivious to the rain and spray now driving in front of the wind. He was thinking of these oil reserves. Fifty times the breakeven figure, at least. Fifty times five hundred thousand million barrels. His brain juggled the figures. Twenty-five million million barrels. Or, as they would say in New York, and they would say it with awe, twenty-five thousand billion barrels.

Commander Gaile met him as he came on board *Circe*. "You're soaked to the skin, Mr. Bright. You'd better get changed. Did you speak to Colney?"

"Yes, he's fine. We had a good chat. By the way, Commander, I haven't had the chance before to thank you for all you've done. It was a remarkable rescue."

"Thank you. It's our job."

"I know, but you really put your heart into it. You and your men. Would it be all right if I arranged for your men to have some rum to keep out this cold and wet?"

"That's very civil of you."

"Good, I'll fix it with Ellam."

"By the way, there's a salvage ship over there. Says she's from Hamburg."

Bright peered through the rain. The big slab-sided ship sprouting heavy lift gear from its decks was lying to, to the south. "I forgot she was on her way. I'll have to go over there later. Maybe you'd come with me, Commander. You could probably put them in the picture better than I could."

"If you wish."

"I've got some messages to send now. I'll see you after that." He turned away and climbed the ladder to the bridge.

Ellam came out of the chartroom when he heard the wheelhouse door. "Lovely weather for the ducks, isn't it. You'll catch your death if you don't get out of those things."

"Why's everyone suddenly concerned about my health?"

"It's just that you're wanted so much. Look here, messages and more messages."

"Let me see."

"I'd better read them to you. My writing's terrible. They were all from some character in London called Ashton." Johnny peered at a scrap of paper. "Yes, this is the first one. Your wife's home and feeling fine. Now, this one says, Pop Hartz sends congratulations. Doesn't say what for. Unless he knows about the third message. Now where's that one. Here it is. Aunt Clara's will proved at four times what you thought. Does that make sense? Have you come into a fortune, Mr. Bright?"

"It doesn't mean what it seems to mean, Johnny. Any coffee?"

"Sure." Ellam got the flask and poured a mug.

"I think I will change into dry things. Keep the R/T open to London, please. I'll need it soon."

Down in Ellam's cabin, Roger stripped and rubbed himself down. The news of Aunt Clara was a shock. Aunt Clara was the private code for one of Inoco's biggest competitors. Aunt Clara had struck gas in the North Sea. That much was common knowledge. The capacity was supposed to be fifty million cubic feet a day. That would be commercial but not spectacular. But if Aunt Clara had flared out on new tests at four times that, that would be spectacular. More important, it made the prospect of gas strikes all the way across to Holland a lot better.

He got into dry clothes and finished the mug of coffee. He went back up to the bridge. He leaned against the bridgefront and stared out of the windows at the rain. *Circe* was riding to one anchor, head to wind. Men were up in the bows hauling in the rope that had held her to the wreck. He asked Ellam for a cigarette and checked his watch. He still had time in hand but what was the use of delaying. Smoke down this cigarette, he decided, then call London.

He weighed the two arguments in his mind as if he was studying horses in the paddock. A two-horse race. Favourite—gas. Outsider—oil from Colney's unique structures.

The Favourite. For. Gas has been struck in healthy quantities in the British sector. Gas is being produced in vast quantities in Holland. Join the British strike and the Dutch gas field with a straight line. Inoco holds leases along that line in the British sector. Piet van Sluys has options on leases along that line in the Dutch sector.

Against. Gas is a nationalised monopoly in Britain. Can a decent price be negotiated? Can the oil companies win the right to pipe their own gas at their own rates to industrial users? Gas is long term, the market is still small. Gas needs new equipment, new capital. The Dutch sector is better. The Dutch encourage the export of gas.

The Outsider. For. Oil has a ready and free market. Oil companies are already equipped to handle and sell oil. A big strike like this in the North Sea could change the whole strategy of world politics. Is that a "for" or an "against"?

Against. There has been no significant strike of oil in the North Sea or in the countries surrounding it. Colney's theory is fantastic. It's all theory. There's not even a trace of oil to support it. Any oilman would hoot at it.

These were the runners but people had to be considered too. There were jockeys, trainers, punters, judges, journalists. They were important.

What about Ted Colney. Is he maybe just a little mad? It's the maddest idea he's had yet. But he was right before. Not always, but often enough. If I turn down the options on his area, what's to stop him going to someone else. Nothing except they'd laugh him out the door.

What about Pop Hartz? How would he feel about the father of his new grandchild spending millions of the company's money and coming up with nothing but salt?

What about the great Roger Bright himself. How would the man fed on success stand up to a monumental failure? But then, how much he would love to make himself a legend with a vast new oil field where everyone else thought the richest harvest was herrings.

The cigarette scorched his fingers. He swore and stubbed it out. He walked over to the radio telephone and asked for Ashton in London.

"Hallo, Harry. Roger here. Yes, yes, everything went very well. Why congratulate me? I just stood and watched. The Navy deserves the credit. And our own crew here on *Circe*, and Captain Ellam. They worked wonders." Johnny swept off his cap and bowed low from the far corner of the wheelhouse. "Yes, Harry, I got all the messages. Quite a surprise about Aunt Clara. Look, is van Sluys standing by in The Hague? Good. Give him a message, please. Tell him to go on to Stage Six. Yes, Stage Six. And tell Paula I'll get home just as soon as I can."

He switched off the set. Even Harry Ashton did not know what Stage Six meant. But Piet van Sluys would know. He would be delighted. He would light a fresh cigar and pour himself a huge Bols and toast Roger in his absence. "I told you so, my boy," he would say. For Stage Six meant that he was to cancel all the options on the areas of Colney's unique structures. Instead he was to take up the options across the southern sector. For once, Roger Bright was backing the favourite.